DOUBLE EDGED BLADE

AN OMEGA THRILLER

BLAKE BANNER

RIGHTHOUSE

ISBN-13: 978-1-63696-334-1

ISBN-10: 1-63696-334-X

Cover design by: Damonza

Printed in the United States of America

www.righthouse.com

www.instagram.com/righthousebooks

www.facebook.com/righthousebooks

twitter.com/righthousebooks

THE OMEGA SERIES

ONE

I<small>T WAS RAINING</small>. F<small>ALL WAS THINKING SERIOUSLY</small> about moving into winter. The rain was steady and a growing mist lingered among naked trunks and branches, saturating the grass and the last rusted leaves. There was a tap at the door behind me. I turned from the leaded window that framed the dank landscape and raised my voice.

"Yes! Come!"

Kenny, my dead father's butler, opened the door and stepped in to my dead father's study. "Mr. Benjamin Smith, sir, and Mr. Jonathan Brown to see you."

"Show them in, Kenny."

He closed the door and I stood looking around at the oak-paneled walls, the heavy, oak desk, the Persian rugs, burgundy chesterfields and the leaded windows: it all reeked of my father. His presence was as strong in death as it had been in life, perhaps stronger. Because now, like the creeping, gray mist outside, it was pervasive and found invisible, hair-line cracks in your resolve, a million invisible ways, to get inside you. I, who had spent my life rejecting and escaping from him, now owned his house, occupied his office, was master of his estate, his legacy.

The door opened again and Kenny admitted the two men. "Mister Smith and Mr. Brown, sir."

They entered in their perfect, anonymous, charcoal gray suits. The door closed behind them and they stood looking at me, without expression. Ben I had met before, when he'd come to my house in Wyoming to tell me my father was dying. He had the bearing and the impassive stare of the professional killer.

Brown was older, maybe in his late forties. His face wasn't ugly, but it was full of ugliness because his expression of contempt had become a habit, a way of life. I watched their eyes travel over my clothes: a khaki army shirt, jeans and boots. I was not in mourning. They attempted to read my face. I made it easy for them.

"You're not welcome here. Say your piece, then leave."

Brown spoke like an android, and for a moment I actually wondered if he was human. "It's not that simple, Mr. Walker."

"I disagree."

"A senior member of Omega has been killed, your own father. That cannot go unpunished. Two other members, Tau and Rho, barely got away with their lives..." He came as close as he was able to an expression. It was a look that suggested he didn't understand why I didn't get him. "You yourself are in possession of information nobody outside Omega has ever had. You must see we can't just walk away..."

I moved to my desk and stared down at the ancient wood. I still thought of it as his desk. I put my ass on it and looked at Brown, at the ingrained expression of contempt that had become a part of what he was.

"There is no 'must' about it, Mr. Brown. It's your problem, not mine."

"I don't think you fully understand, Mr. Walker. We are offering you your father's position in Omega. You will step in as Gamma, a member of the Cabal of Five. Nobody has ever entered directly into the Cabal of Five."

"I know what you're offering me, Mr. Brown, and I know why. You're offering me that position in the government within the government, because the Cabal is scared of me. They are right to be scared of me, and both of you would be wise to be scared of me too, because I am running out of patience."

Ben looked vaguely amused.

"Lacklan, you know that we will come after you and Marni, and we will kill you if you don't accept this offer. This is your one chance to state your terms." He gave a small shrug. "Shape Omega from the inside if you want. We don't have to be enemies."

I knew now that my father had tried that. He had told me on his death bed. And I knew how it had played out. He had become a bitter, twisted killer. That was what Omega did to you. I could have argued with them, tried to tell them that you can never shape that kind of power from the inside. You just get consumed and shaped by it, into something infirm, ugly and contemptuous, like Mr. Brown, like my father. But arguing with them was as pointless as arguing with the pervasive mist outside. They were what they were, an expression of the dark, monstrous face of nature; humanity at its worst.

"You've said your piece, you've done what you came here to do. Now leave. And tell the Cabal that if they think they are coming after me, they are wrong. I am coming after them."

Ben shook his head and actually looked sad. "Last chance, Lacklan."

"There are twenty-four letters in the ancient Greek alphabet, Ben, one for each member of Omega. That's twenty-four kills I am going to make. I am guessing you two are messengers, lackeys, so that's twenty-six including you." I paused for my words to sink in, then added, "As of this moment, your lives are at risk. My advice is, leave. Now."

Brown nodded and they moved to the door. Ben paused to look back at me before he left. "It's a shame," he said, "I like you."

THE SMALL CHURCH was less than three hundred yards away as the crow flies, through the woods, but the procession followed the prescribed route up the drive to Concord Road, then down Sudbury road to St George's. It was a half-mile walk all told, enveloped in mist and drizzle, following the hearse. There were a lot of people I didn't know. I wondered if any of them were from Omega, but I doubted it.

We sat through the service, which was my father's last great act of hypocrisy, as he had been an atheist from the age of twelve. But to him, the social structures of the establishment, from the golf club to the church, were sources of power, and he had to be a part of them to use them.

The pastor had asked me if I wanted to give a eulogy. I

told him I didn't. I had hated my father all my adult life. It was that hatred that had driven me to move to England and spend ten years training as a killer with the British SAS, and destroyed my relationship with Marni. It was true I had discovered a different man in him on the day he died, but that discovery was something between him and me, and that was how it was going to stay.

I'd contacted my mother in England, told her her husband had died, as had Bob, her son. I didn't tell her the details. I didn't tell her that Marni, who had been like a surrogate daughter to her, had shot Robert, my father. I didn't tell her that I had thrown Bob, her son, my brother, off a roof and broken his neck. I just asked her if she wanted to come to the funeral. Her reply was brief and to the point; ice cold in that way only the English know how. She told me that as far as she was concerned, they had both died a long time ago, and she invited me to visit her in England as soon as I could.

So I sat in the ancient church and listened to the pastor commit my father's soul to a God in whom he did not believe, in a heaven he did not deserve to occupy, and praise him for his acts of goodness and kindness towards humanity, a species he had conspired to decimate and enslave.

His coffin was then carried out across the wet grass, through the lingering mist, among the twisted, gray fingers of the dead trees, to his grave: a gash of red earth in the green turf, among the tilted headstones of twelve generations of Walkers.

He was lowered into the ground, watched by a chorus of black figures under shining black umbrellas that tapped out a wet, irregular rhythm of winter and death. The pastor said a last few words and somebody handed me a spade. I didn't want a spade. I stepped over, took a handful of mud and stood looking down at the cask. Most of my life I had hated him, and the scar of that hatred had disfigured me. Now, in death, the most he could give me was a feeling of deep confusion. Maybe that was the most any of us could give each other. I threw the mud onto his coffin and bid him goodbye.

People I didn't know, but seemed to know me, filed past, shaking my hand and telling me how sorry they were. The crowd began to thin and the jostling umbrellas began to disperse. That was when I saw her. She was about fifty feet away, maybe a little less, standing in the shelter of a tree. Like me, she wasn't wearing mourning. She was dressed in jeans, a long, oiled leather coat, and a leather hat. When she saw that I had seen her, she turned and started walking away through the trees, toward Concord Road.

The remaining few mourners must have thought I was crazy, but if they knew my father, that was probably what they expected of me. I muttered an excuse and ran. I circled the grave where two men were shoveling in the dirt and sprinted through the mud toward the trees. By the time I got to the copse where she'd been standing, she had disappeared. I stumbled down the bank, through the slippery, dead leaves and saturated turf, grabbing at the tree trunks for support, and glimpsed her, thirty yards ahead of me, down by the road. There was a bleep and a flash as she unlocked her car. I scrambled, not wanting to shout her name in case somebody from Omega was there, in case Ben or Brown were still around.

I heard the door slam and shouted, "*Wait! I need to talk to you!*"

She pulled away as I exploded from the trees onto the glistening blacktop. The car was nondescript, a gray Ford Focus. I took a mental snapshot of the plate just before she disappeared from view toward Weston, and Boston.

It was an Arizona registration.

I made my way back to the house through the woods, avoiding the road, asking myself why the hell she had come to his funeral. To gloat? To repent? The Marni I had known would never gloat, but then the Marni I had known would not have killed a man either. Hatred can etch deep changes into a person. I didn't know who she was anymore, and that gave me a sick pit in my belly.

I hadn't arranged for people to come back and drink and celebrate his life. His life was not something I thought should be celebrated. They could do that on their own time and their own dollar. Instead I had a hot shower, changed my clothes and told Kenny to bring some lunch to the study. He had a fire burning in there and as I closed the door and sat at the desk, for a moment I was surprised to realize it almost felt like home.

I dismissed the thought and switched on my laptop. Fifteen minutes on Google told me that the gray Ford Focus belonged to Sarah Connors. I smiled. Cute. We had both loved that movie. The address, on East 26th Street, in Alvernon Heights, Tucson, was probably fake, like the name. But with fake names and addresses, like any kind of lie, it pays to stay as close to the truth as possible, and she knew that. My gut said she was in Tucson.

Had she come in spite of me? Or had she come here because she wanted me to know it, too?

There was a tap at the door and Kenny came in with a

tray of cheese, pickles and warm bread. There was also a bottle of English bitter. You can keep your Belgian and your German and Czech. Real beer is made in the north of England. It's man's drink, and it is drunk at room temperature. That's just the way it is.

When I'd finished the cheese, I sat drinking the beer, smoking a Pueblo cigarette and gazing into the hot coals. However much I wanted to, I couldn't second-guess her. The name she'd chosen to register the car, like the photograph she'd pinned to the board in the kitchen when she'd first disappeared and my father had asked me to find her, suggested she wanted me to know where she'd gone. But I kept coming up against the same anxiety, over and again. This was a different Marni. I didn't know this Marni anymore. I had watched her kill my father, a man whom she had loved. I didn't know what her motivation was, or what she was capable of.

She was pursuing her father's research, research that could bring Omega down, research that had driven Omega to order my father to kill him. I had exposed that truth to her, and now that she knew it, it was impossible to know how deep her desire for vengeance went, or what lengths she was prepared to go to. Yet, my father's dying wish had been that I should protect her.

I made my way up to my bedroom, pulled my old army rucksack from the wardrobe, and threw it on the bed. I opened my gun cupboard and thought about the weapons I might need. I wasn't going into the wilds, I wasn't going to be blowing anything up, all I needed was my Sig Sauer p226 and two extended magazines. I threw in the silencer, the telescopic sight with night vision, and my night vision goggles. I stared at the Smith & Wesson 500, decided against it and chucked it in anyway, because you never know when you're going to have to stop a bus. I threw in a couple of tablets of C4 and a few detonators too, remote and universal for good measure.

Let's face it, in life you never know what you are going to need.

Then I opened my tech cupboard and took out half a dozen tracking devices and a couple of listening bugs, plus my pack of lock picks. Those I had a hunch I would need.

I wrapped it all in a pair of jeans, a couple of shirts and a handful of socks, and slung it over my shoulder. Then I went down to the kitchen to talk to Kenny and Rosalia.

It was warm in there and smelled of baking.

"Should we expect you back at any particular time, sir?"

"I don't know, Kenny. Maybe a week, maybe a little longer. I'll keep you posted. Anyone calls, I've gone to Canada for the week."

Rosalia grabbed my face and gave me two huge kisses. "You gonna be careful! You take care don' do nothin' crazy! OK?"

I smiled. "I'll do my best, Rosalia."

I gave her a kiss, shook hands with Kenny, and stepped out into the mist and the drizzle. The taxi cab was waiting in the drive. I climbed in the back and slammed the door. The driver looked at me in the mirror.

"Where to?"

I knew that if she drove non-stop it would take her almost two days to get to Tucson. I could do it in a lot less than that in my customized Zombie 222. But the Zombie was a car that got noticed, and for the moment, whether

Marni wanted me to follow her or not, I didn't want her to know I was there. The Greyhound would get me to Tucson in just over two and a half days. That suited me fine.

"The Greyhound Bus Station on Atlantic Avenue, in Boston."

"You got it."

TWO

Two and a half days on the bus gave me plenty of time to find a guest house. I wound up at Cissy's on Avenida Fria, in the Presidio district. In early October in Arizona, it's still warm during daylight hours. As I climbed out of my rental car and stood on the broad front porch that afternoon, with the desert hills behind me, I figured we were hitting eighty-five degrees under a perfect blue sky. It made a change from Massachusetts.

The door opened and a pretty blond with freckles and mischievous eyes smiled and raised an eyebrow at me. I smiled right back.

"Are you Cissy?"

"Are you?"

"Not last time I checked, but sixty-four hours on a Greyhound bus can do things to a man. You think we ought to check?"

Her laugh was as cute as her face. She moved aside and let me in.

"I think I'd better not. I could get into trouble!"

I stepped inside. "I won't tell if you don't."

She led me upstairs to my room. It was plain, simple and comfortable, with a bed, a desk, and a chair. She leaned on the door jamb as I dumped my rucksack and looked around.

"The rent covers bed and breakfast. You're my only guest right now, so I can make lunch and dinner too, but that's extra and you eat what I eat. There ain't no menu a la carte. And Saturdays Red sometimes comes over for dinner, that's my boyfriend, and if he does, then we eat alone."

"Lucky Red." I took out my wallet and gave her a thousand dollars. Her eyes went wide as she took them and counted them. "Tell me when that runs out. I'll try not to be around when Red visits. I'll join you for dinner tonight. Steak and French fries will do fine. And a cold beer."

She gave me a once over that had more amusement than annoyance in it. "I told you, you eat what I eat."

"Then I guess tonight you're eating steak and fries. About seven will be great." I smiled nicely. "Now I need to do some work."

She giggled her pretty giggle. "You are going to be *fun* to have around, mister."

"I hope you won't even notice me."

She raised an eyebrow and gave me a 'really?' look. "You better hope Red don't notice you. He's the jealous type."

She left and I closed the door. I took my laptop from my bag and put it on the desk. I'd had plenty of time to think through what I wanted to do, and I'd come to the conclusion there were too many variables and too many uncertainties. What I needed was information; information about who Marni had become, and what she was about. So I spent the next half hour putting classified ads in the local papers and in the *New York Times*, a paper I knew she read every day. The ad said simply: 'You were right about Robert the first time. I was wrong. He was misunderstood. We need to talk.'

While I had always hated my father, she had loved him. He had cared for her since she was a small child, almost as his own daughter, tortured by the guilt of having murdered her father, his own best friend. Now that she knew that, because I had told her, our roles had reversed. I saw him as a pathetic, tortured human being, and she saw him as a monster. The ad might draw a response.

It was a long shot. But Marni was nothing if not smart. She had known I would see her at the funeral. She knew me well enough to know I would memorize her license plate and track her to Tucson. And that meant just one thing: that was what she had wanted me to do. It followed logically, then, that I would use the classified ads to try to contact her.

It didn't mean I was here. It just meant I knew that she was.

At seven, I went down. Cissy had an open-plan living room and dining room, separated from the kitchen by a breakfast bar. The table was set for two and she was in the kitchen. I could hear the potatoes sizzling in the deep fryer. I went and leaned on the bar. I could see a plate by the cooker with two large steaks on it.

She glanced at me and smiled.

I said, "I hope I didn't put you to too much inconvenience, Cissy."

"Uh-uh. So happens I was having steak anyhow. You want your beer now, or later with your meal?"

"I want one now and another with my meal."

"This ain't a bar, you know!"

"But you'll make an exception for me."

"And just how do you figure that?"

I paused long enough to smile and get her to smile back. "I'm an expert in the ancient art of freckle reading, and I can read you like a book."

Her eyes creased and she giggled, and pulled two beers from the fridge. As she cracked them and handed me one, I saw a flash of real concern in her eyes. It was there for just a second, but I caught it.

"Don't go saying things like that in front of Red, you hear?"

I took a swig. "I don't plan to cause any problems, Cissy. I don't plan to stay long enough."

She didn't say anything. She went over to check the fries. They were about right, so she lit the gas under the steak griddle. After a moment, I said, "You know something I learned, a long time ago?"

She answered without looking at me. "Of course not."

"I learned that if there is somebody in your life who is scaring you, there is only one thing you can do." She gave me a glance that said she didn't like where I was going, but was curious all the same. I went on. I went on because I didn't care whether she liked it or not. "The only thing you can do is cut off their nuts and nail their scrotum to their foreheads. After that they stop scaring you."

Her laughter was more like a shriek. She stamped her foot, screwed up her eyes and shook her head, but she didn't answer until we were both sitting down at the table and she had given me a second beer. Then she wagged her fork at me and spoke through a full mouth.

"You go through life like that, you're gonna get into big trouble, mister."

I shrugged and ate in silence for a moment. The steak was good.

"I try to stay out of trouble, Cissy." I smiled and quoted, "'Don't go looking for trouble if trouble ain't lookin' to be looked for.' But sometimes trouble comes knocking at your door. What do you do? Lie down and let it walk all over you?"

Her smile faded and she concentrated on her food for a moment. "I guess that's what I do. My mommy always taught me, you gotta placate men. It's only worse if you stand up to them."

"Really? And how did that work for her?"

She put a smile on the left side of her face, where it didn't really look like a smile. "Not so good, I suppose."

"It's like candy. The more you give a kid candy, the more they want. The more you placate a bully, the more he'll keep bullying you. Cut off his nuts, problem solved."

"Let's talk about somethin' else. This talk makes me sad."

It wasn't hard. She was a chatterbox and it was easy for me to sit back and listen. Eventually, she cleared the plates and washed them while I leaned on the bar and finished my beer. As she put the plates in the rack to dry, she asked me, "You wanna watch a movie?"

But before I could answer, the doorbell rang. The look she gave me was more eloquent than a thousand words. It was a look of fear, and of pleading. It said, "Don't make a scene, don't flirt, don't upset him. Just go."

She took my bottle from my hand and put it in the recycling bin, then went to open the door. She greeted him effusively. He ignored her, stepping into the room staring at me. He was six-two and powerfully built, with a platinum crew cut and pale blue eyes. His face said he wanted to know who the hell I was.

Cissy was drawing breath to explain. I knew his type, and I knew any explanation she gave him would just make him mad. So I smiled and stepped forward, holding out my hand.

"You must be Red. I'm Lacklan, the new lodger. I'll be here just a couple of days." I upgraded the smile to a grin. "Cissy has been telling me all about her man. I was just heading up to my room, so I guess I'll leave you two in peace."

The hostility in his eyes shifted to a smug smile and he took my hand.

"That's considerate of you..." He frowned. "Lacklan? What kind of a name is that? I guess you're from out east, huh? What's your business here, Lacklan?"

Some obscure motivation I did not understand at the time made me answer without thinking. "Well, I'm looking for work, as it happens. Things are not so good in New York, so I thought I'd make a new start in Arizona."

He studied me for a second. "What kind of work you looking for?"

I shrugged. "I was in the army from the age of nineteen, so I'll do pretty much anything."

He gave a single nod. His eyes were calculating and his

mouth was hanging slightly open. A right cross would have smashed his jaw. I put the thought out of my mind, told myself not to get involved in their business and made to move toward the stairs. But he spoke before I could leave.

"Seen action?"

I nodded. "Some."

"Where?"

"Iraq, Afghanistan..." There were other places, but they were places I wouldn't talk about, SAS black ops that were more than secret.

There was the trace of a sneer on his face. "You good at taking orders?"

I averted my eyes so he wouldn't see how close he was to spending the rest of the week in hospital. "I followed orders for over ten years. I figure that's enough." I made a friendly face and pointed a finger at him, like a gun. "You guys have a nice evening."

I headed for the stairs. I could feel his eyes on my back. He called after me. "I'll keep my eyes open. Let you know if I hear of anything."

"Appreciate it."

I LAY IN BED, in the dark, staring at the eerie light of the moon setting over the desert in the west. It filtered through my open window, along with a cool breeze that moved the lace curtains, whispering about predators in the night. Far off, you could hear the wild cry of the coyotes, baying into the turquoise half-light. And for a while there was an owl who seemed to be warning of trouble.

Downstairs I could hear Cissy and Red. They started out

with the Eagles, laughing, dancing, singing along to Hotel California. Then, after a few tequilas, she must have said something he chose to misunderstand, something that offended his manhood and went contrary to his rules about men and women and life. And the more she tried to explain and to placate him, the madder he got. Because there was only one thing that was going to satisfy him.

At first I told myself not to get involved. It was none of my business. I had a job to do. I was looking for Marni, and I had to stay focused. But after the third slap, I knew I had no choice, and I got up and pulled on my jeans. By then he'd slapped her six times and I knew I was going to break his arm so he would never slap anybody again.

By the time I'd reached the door she was sobbing and apologizing, and telling him she loved him and only him and there was no other man in the world who came close. He was her man.

"I love you baby, you know that."

I stood on the landing, a hot pellet of rage in my belly. Now he was lecturing her, telling her that he loved her, but she had to learn to talk right, and think about the things she said, so as not to upset him. And then he was kissing her noisily. I turned and went back into my room. I lay in the dark, and for the next fifteen minutes tried to listen to the coyotes, while Red and Cissy made love on the couch to the sound of Lying Eyes.

That's what you call irony.

THREE

I GOT UP LATE, AT NINE O'CLOCK, SHOWERED AND dressed and went downstairs for nine-thirty. She was in the kitchen washing a cup in the sink and didn't look round when I leaned on the breakfast bar.

"Breakfast is at eight. I should have told you. I can't be making breakfast all day, dependin' what time you feel like getting up."

She delivered the whole speech looking down into the sink.

When she'd finished, I said, "My breakfast is at six-thirty and I make it myself. I'm up late because you and Red kept me awake till four in the morning with the racket you were making."

She was silent, motionless, still staring into the sink. When she finally spoke, there was a catch in her voice. "If you don't like it, there's plenty of other places you can go."

"That suits me fine, Cissy. Take what I owe you for last night and give me my thousand dollars back." I waited. She was swaying slightly and I knew she was crying. "You can't, can you? Because Red took it last night."

"That ain't none of your business."

"It is if you're kicking me out, because that money is not yours or his. It's mine."

She hunched forward and made a strange, strangled noise. I went around the bar and stood behind her at the sink. She was sobbing convulsively. I put my hands on her shoulders and turned her around. She covered her face, but the bruises were clearly visible. She leaned against my chest so I couldn't see them.

I put my arms around her and sighed, telling myself I didn't need this kind of complication.

"Where is he?"

She looked up at me in alarm and I saw the full extent of the damage he'd done. Her left eye was swollen and her right cheek was purple and turning to yellow. I've seen enough bruised faces in my life to know that left eyes get bruised and swollen from right jabs, and right cheeks get bruised from backhanders.

"Why d'you wanna know?"

"Because I am going to break his arms so that he never hits another woman as long as he lives." I said it without feeling or inflection. It was a simple fact.

She shook her head. "Don't get involved. It's not your business." She pulled away from me and went to get the coffee pot. "He won't be back till Saturday, and he'll be OK now for a few weeks. He only does this like once a month..."

She spoke in a rush, her hands shaking as she put the filter in the jug and spilled grains into it. I could feel hot anger rising inside me again.

"*What?*"

"He gets real stressed at work and it makes him crazy sometimes. He don't want to get violent. He don't mean it. I wind him up sometimes. I don't think before I speak..."

"Stop." She turned and stared at me with wide eyes. "Listen to yourself. Why are you making excuses for him?"

She looked away and put the coffee on to brew. "He ain't so bad..."

"Cissy."

She looked away, biting her lip.

"Why do you let him do this to you?"

"That ain't none of your business. You ain't got no right prying..."

I frowned. "So let me get this straight. He doesn't need permission to beat you up, but I need permission to care that he does."

She ignored me, went and stood looking down at the cooker. After a moment, she said, "You want pancakes? Bacon?"

"Just a piece of toast."

"You mad?" She turned frightened eyes on me. "Don't be mad. I couldn't take another scene."

I shook my head. "Don't play that game, Cissy. I'll respect your wishes—for now. But next time he keeps me awake, I'm going to drag him upstairs and throw him out the window."

She gave a nervous smile. "That'd be something to watch."

I didn't return the smile. "You think you haven't got a choice, Cissy, but you have."

She brought my coffee and my toast to the table and sat

with me. After a bit she said, "I'm sorry you couldn't sleep. Must have been unpleasant."

"Where does he work?"

"You're not going to…"

"No. I told you I'd respect your wishes. He said he might be able to get me a job."

"Oh." She seemed a bit disappointed. "Him and his partner, Chetan, they got a club out on Camino del Oeste."

"Chetan?"

"He's Indian—sorry—Native American. They started a club together. He's there most nights. Sometimes it gets a bit rough, so I know he was looking for somebody to keep an eye on things." She looked uncomfortable. "But there's plenty other work you could do."

"That where he'll be tonight?" She nodded. I drained my cup. "I have to go out now. I'll probably be out most of the day, but I figure I'll be back by six, for dinner. Then I'll go visit Red's club."

I left her sitting at the table, staring into her coffee.

I took Los Reales to the I-19 and then drove north for ten minutes till I came to the West Speedway Boulevard. That took me as far as the University of Arizona, where I parked outside the School of Natural Resources and the Environment.

A little research over the previous couple of days had told me that Professor Richard Engels, of the University of Arizona, was a world authority on climate change and sustainable resources. I didn't believe that it was a coincidence that Marni had come here. I knew she had come here for a reason, and I suspected that the reason was to see Engels. Five minutes on the university website had given me a photograph of him, but I wanted to see him in person.

I made my way to reception and stood for a moment looking lost while people milled around me. Pretty soon I saw a woman who didn't look like a student. She was in a hurry, but had a friendly face. I intercepted her apologetically and said, "Excuse me, I'm kind of lost. Can you tell me where Professor Engels' lecture is?"

She looked a little confused, but she was basically a nice person so she smiled and said, "Well sure..." She glanced at her watch. "It'll be in the... um... lecture theater..." She pointed me in the right direction and said, "You are very late, though. He'll be finishing. Are you a student?"

I grimaced and said, "I hope so," and hurried away.

I found the lecture theater, slipped in and sat right at the back where I hoped I would be invisible. It was an amphitheater design and the room was pretty full. Professor Engels was in his mid-fifties, tall and strongly built. He had a lot of black hair, turning to gray, which he had tied back in a ponytail. He had a powerful voice too, that carried.

"... So, we really need to be changing the debate. The question is no longer, whose *fault* is climate change. Nor is it, what can we do to *stop* climate change. Both of those questions have become redundant. Whatever the government, or the IPCC for that matter, may be telling you about the changing climate of our planet, the data, the *facts*, tell us *beyond any conceivable doubt*, that we have gone past the tipping point." He paused, took four slow steps to his left and four slow steps back. Then his voice boomed, "*It is too late! There is no way back!*" He paused again, then used his hands to emphasize what he was saying. "Over the next twenty years, the world is going to change beyond all recognition, and the question we need to be asking is, *what do we need to do to be able to adapt and survive in the new environment?*"

He held up his right hand with his fingers splayed. "What are the five defining elements of this new environment?"

He waited. Nobody answered so he held up his thumb. "Heat! The world will be hot. Many places that are today super-producers of food, will be too hot to produce any food at all. Which brings us to number two: barren. Ninety percent of the world will be non-productive. Very small areas of the far north will be fertile, but tropical and subtropical areas will be too hot, too windy, too dry and/or, too wet... Too much of everything. Barren. *Non*-productive."

He held up thumb, index and middle finger. "Three: hostile. The environment will be *extreme*, in violent, chaotic readjustment. The human being is a fragile animal and needs a stable environment in which to prosper. The environment of the twenty-first century will be unstable, unbalanced, chaotic and *extreme*. Extreme, spiraling heat will bring not just hurricanes and tropical storms, but also winters of *extreme cold*. We will see weather systems of *extreme* proportions moving chaotically across the globe at violent speeds well in excess of a hundred MPH."

He held up his hand with his thumb flattened against his palm. "Four, and this is a really important one: *overpopulated!* We are rapidly and exponentially approaching the limit of what the planet can sustain..." He paused, staring at his audience, and then bellowed suddenly, *"In optimum, industrialized conditions!* But cripple industry, cripple mass production and mass distribution, and crank up the temperatures in the great factory farms of the world, throw in drought and torrential flooding, and how do we support *eight or nine billion people?*

"What happens then? What do these people do, who are losing their land and their livelihood? They do what they have done throughout history. They migrate and take their neighbor's land.

"So overpopulation means mass and aggressive migration, climate refugees, thousand of millions of people depending on ever shrinking agriculturally productive areas..." He held up his hand again with his five fingers splayed wide. "And that brings us to number five. War. War for resources. War for control of resources. And let me tell you, that war has already begun..."

He didn't explain his last comment. He wrapped up the talk and his students started filing out. I made my way down the steps and joined him at his desk, where he was dumping books into an old leather bag. He frowned at me as I approached. His tone was blunt but not unfriendly.

"Who are you?"

I thought about the question for a moment while he watched me. "What would you say," I asked, "if I said I represented Omega, and advised you to refrain from the meeting you are planning."

His face flushed and his eyes blazed. "I'd tell you to go to hell and stop harassing me! God damn it! Who in the hell do you think...!"

I raised my hand. He stopped talking, looked at my hand and then at my face, like he thought I was crazy. I said, "Has she been in touch yet?"

"What? *Who?*"

"Marni Gilbert."

"Yes... Who the hell are you?"

I stepped closer to him and studied his face. He looked sincere. He looked like a pain in the ass, but a good man. "Be careful. These people are dangerous. They *will* kill you. They killed her father. They are ruthless. Do you understand me? Ask her what happened to her father." I shook my head. "You're a smart man, Professor, but you're at risk. You're both at risk. You're both out of your depth. Tell her that."

I left. I looked back down at him when I got to the door. He still had a book in his hand and he was still staring at me.

I went back into the bright glare of the late morning sun and sat in my car for a bit, watching the entrance. I pulled out a Pueblo cigarette, flipped my brass Zippo and leaned into the flame. I was trying to work out if what I had done was stupid or smart. It had been spontaneous and instinctual. I inhaled deeply and blew smoke out the window. I'd seen men like Engels before. They were brave, idealistic loud mouths, and mostly they were dead too. From the way he'd answered my first query, Omega had already been in touch with him. I knew if he kept mouthing off, sooner or later they'd come for him. And if Marni was trying to hook up with him, she would be at risk also. What I needed to do was persuade her, through him, to talk to me. From what I could see, they were both going off half-cocked and had no system, no plan. And they were both going to get each other killed.

I waited an hour and smoked four cigarettes. Finally, I saw him come out. He stood on the steps and scanned the area for a while, probably looking for me. Finally, he made his way to a Buick and climbed in. I made a mental note of the plate and watched him pull away. When he was almost out of sight, I followed.

I followed him onto the East Speedway Boulevard. He turned east and kept going straight for about ten minutes, till he came to North Kolb Road, where he turned south. There were low, flat buildings, tall thin palms and pale ochre dust as far as the eye could see, all under a glaring, white-blue sky. He kept going for about five minutes or more and finally turned left on Stella Road.

I turned in after him and slowed to keep my distance. He turned left into Cordova and then right into Brooks Drive. I parked and watched him pull into a driveway three hundred yards down the road, beside a gray Ford Focus.

I waited twenty minutes and saw him come out again, climb into his car and head back toward the university. I waited another ten minutes and moved closer, till I had a clear view of the house. Then I phoned Domino's and ordered a pizza, to be delivered to her address. I had time to smoke two more cigarettes before the guy on the scooter arrived. She opened the door herself. I sighed. It was a miracle she had survived as long as she had. They argued for a bit. I figured she was telling him she hadn't ordered the damn pizza. Finally she took it, paid him and he went on his way.

So now I knew where she was and why she was here. Or at least, I was pretty sure I knew. Now the question was, what was I going to do with that information?

And I hadn't a clue.

FOUR

I KNEW THAT IF I APPROACHED HER DIRECTLY, SHE would bolt. I didn't know why, but just as in Turret, Colorado, it seemed she wanted to let me know where she was and what she was doing—she wanted me to be there—but she was determined not to make direct contact. For the moment I just had to play her game and accept that was the way she wanted to operate.

I stared out at the glaring sunshine, at the bizarre cactus gardens and the tall, thin palms against the stark blue sky. The stillness was almost oppressive. I drummed my fingers on the wheel and tried to concentrate.

What had been the purpose of Engel's visit? Had I scared him off? Had he come to tell her that he wanted no more contact with her? Knowing his type, I decided that was unlikely. If anything, he would have interpreted my warning as a threat, and that would have spurred him on to greater bravado.

What then? He had come to pass on the warning; to tell

her that Omega knew about her presence in Tucson, about her contacting him. To tell her they had sent somebody to threaten him. Would she guess it was me? Maybe. She was IQ smart, academic smart, but she wasn't street smart or survival smart.

For a moment, I felt the impulse to march in, grab her by the shoulders, and try to shake some sense into her, but I stopped myself. Instead, I sat and watched the house for the next five hours. As dusk closed in, I saw her pull the drapes and shut out the light from inside. I got out of my car and covered the distance to her Focus at a silent run. I reached in my pocket and pulled out one of the tracking devices I had brought with me, slipped it under the chassis, heard the satisfying magnetic clunk, and returned to my car. I sat a moment and checked the receiver. It was working well. At least if she drove anywhere I'd be able to follow her. It was a start.

I turned the car around and headed back to Cissy's place. I had Marni covered, at least partially and provisionally. Now it was time to go and have a chat with Red. Whatever I had told Cissy, I planned to scare the living daylights out of him. And if that wasn't enough, I'd break a few damned bones. One thing was for certain. After tonight, he wouldn't be beating anybody up again in a hurry.

CISSY and I ate in almost total silence. I guess she had a bad combination of bruising, lack of sleep and a tequila hangover. When we'd finished, she muttered, "Goodnight," and went up to bed. I gave her five minutes and went up to my room. I put on my shoulder holster under my jacket, slipped in the Sig with the regular magazine and put my Fairbairn & Sykes double-edged SAS fighting knife in my boot. I didn't figure I'd need any more than that. Not tonight.

I went down to my car and drove out toward the desert.

Cissy had told me where the club was. It was called the Hawk's Nest and it was about two miles south, on Camino del Oeste, on the edge of town. It was a one-storey building set back thirty feet from the road, with a 1950s style neon sign over the door that spelled out the name in green and red, with a picture of a hawk instead of an apostrophe between the 'k' and the 's'. It looked unearthly against the night sky.

There were a dozen Harleys parked in the forecourt, and a similar number of pick-ups. I could hear the throb of music from inside: a wholesome woman singing about how she missed her man, to the whine of a slide guitar. I crossed the lot and pushed through the door.

The place was warm and noisy. It was a basic concrete box, with wooden rafters and a couple of cartwheels on the walls. The air was thick with tobacco smoke, talk, and laughter, overlaid with Lady Antebellum howling about just one kiss. It was full, and as the vehicles outside had suggested, about half the patrons were bikers and Angels, and the other half were rednecks. I have nothing against either. And if I ever had to trust my life to anybody, I'd sooner pick a redneck than a preacher, any day of the week.

I pushed through the crowd and leaned on the bar. The guy who stepped up to serve me was six-three and had a face like a roadmap of the dark side of life. He was native American Indian or Mexican, and had long hair tied in a ponytail. It went all the way down to the big knife he had in his waistband behind his back. He didn't ask me what I wanted, he jerked his chin at me.

"Is Red in?" The shake of his head was barely perceptible. "Give me a beer."

He went away to get a bottle from the fridge. He cracked it and put it in front of me. "What you want with Red?"

"He said he might have a job for me."

His eyes gave me a quick once-over. "Kind of job?"

"I don't know. That's why I'm here."

He pulled a face and shrugged in a way that suggested he couldn't even be bothered to pull a face and shrug. Then he walked away. I found a table that gave me a view of the bar and I sat down to wait. It wasn't long before a pretty Mexican girl came and sat next to me.

"Hey, I'm Lucia. You all alone tonight?"

I nodded. "Yup. And that's how I aim to stay."

My tone wasn't hostile so she didn't go away. She pouted instead. "Aw, you ain't real friendly!"

"It's nothing personal. I have business tonight."

Her eyes lit up at the word and she leaned forward. "What kind of business?"

I smiled all over the right side of my face. "The kind that's none of yours."

She grinned. "Blow? You got some? We can party for free if you got some blow."

I shook my head. "Not tonight."

She sagged and suddenly looked bored. "At least buy a girl a drink."

"Who's the guy behind the bar?"

"Chetan? That's Red's partner. He's a mean son of a bitch."

I gave her ten bucks. "Have a drink. We'll party some other night. Where's Red?"

She took the bill without comment. "What's tonight, Tuesday? He'll be at the border tonight, and Friday."

"What's at the border?"

She raised a perfect eyebrow at me. "You ask a lot of questions, mister."

"Yeah? Information is power. Didn't you know that?"

She pointed a finger at me. "You better be careful. That kind of talk can get you hurt around these parts."

I watched her walk up to the bar, looking for somebody who might be looking for her. Then I looked around with more interest. Lucia was obviously part of what was on offer here, and as I scanned the place I began to see more girls who were selling their services. There were maybe six of them, all Mexican, all cute. So Red and Chetan ran a brothel with Mexican whores. Maybe the job he wanted to offer me was muscle to protect his girls. But I couldn't help wondering, while I sat there and waited, what he was doing at the border. Collecting more girls? How many did he need?

Then I remembered how Lucia had reacted when I'd said I was there on business. Her automatic response was to assume it was blow. So Red was running whores and cocaine. He was as unoriginal as he was stupid.

Up at the bar, Lucia was talking to six Angels. They were laughing a lot and a couple of them kept groping her. She was laughing back and slapping their hands. I couldn't hear her but she was clearly saying, don't handle the goods till you've paid. Things got a little physical and Chetan strolled up. There was some talk. Money changed hands and three of the Angels went out back with Lucia. She glanced at me as she passed and I saw fear in her eyes. Not panic. Just a little fear.

Shit happens.

Twenty minutes went by. During that time I saw a few guys snorting coke. I couldn't see where they were getting it, but it was clear this was a joint where the cops didn't drop in unannounced. I wondered if Chetan was selling it behind the bar. I guessed he was, but I didn't see anything to confirm it.

The three Angels came back in one by one, looking smug, like they'd done something smart that nobody else could do. When the last one was in, Lucia didn't follow, and from the mimes and the laughter that was going down at the bar I could figure why. She'd made a lot of money tonight, but she'd spend a week nursing the bruises. It occurred to me that these were the people—this was the humanity—that Marni and Engels were trying so hard to save.

But who was I to judge?

That was when Red came in. I watched him walk to the bar, slap a few backs, laugh, and then exchange a nod and a couple of words with Chetan. Chetan jerked his head in my direction and Red turned, saw me and narrowed his eyes. He said something to his partner, who gave him a bottle of beer, and he brought it over to my table and sat down.

"You get around, mister. Every time I look, there y'are."

I let him finish and counted to three slowly before I answered. "You said you might have a job for me. I thought I'd drop in and say hello."

He shook his head. "I said I'd keep my eyes open. That ain't the same thing."

"Have you got a job for me?"

"Nope."

"Are you sure?"

His pale blue eyes said he was getting pissed. "I just got through telling you..."

I sat forward and put my elbows on the table. I looked him in the eye and nodded toward the Angels at the bar. "See those six guys there? They just put one of your girls out of action for a week at least. I don't know how much they paid her, but I'm willing to bet it's not as much as she'll make for you over seven nights."

His expression changed. I was talking his language. He shrugged. "Things get hot here and sometimes the girls get hurt. It's the way it goes." He laughed like he thought I was stupid. "Besides, those are Angels. You don't say no to the Angels."

"You're scared of the Angels?" He didn't like that. I didn't give a damn. I'd come here to break both his arms, but now I was thinking I might go a little further. "Who else you scared of? You're doing business down at the border, that means you're treading on somebody's toes. I figure you're treading on Mexican toes."

"You got a big mouth, boy."

I spoke real quiet. "Pick the most dangerous man in this bar, Red. I'm going to break the fingers of his left hand. Then I'll break his right elbow. After that I'll break his left knee. Then I'll break his neck; and after that I'll kill his best friend. If I do that, will you give me a job?"

I could see contempt and fear fighting for dominance on his face. Confusion trumped them both. "You kill anyone in this bar, boy, an' I'll shoot you myself, like a mad dog. You want to impress me, get the goddamn Mexicans off my back. Meantime, get the hell out of my club. I don't like you."

I smiled. "You will."

And it would be the biggest mistake he ever made. The most dangerous man in the bar, apart from me, was Chetan, and Red was his best friend. And I planned to make good on my promise. I stood.

"Be seeing you, Red."

FIVE

I WAS UP AT FIVE AND WENT FOR A RUN IN THE desert. It was dark and real cold, and the stars were like shards of ice. I trained for an hour and then ran back. Had a cold shower and went down for breakfast at half past seven. Cissy was up and in the kitchen making coffee. She gave me a smile that was as real as canned laughter.

"Mornin'! You were up early! How'd it go last night? Red offer you a job?"

"Nope."

"Aww...! That's a shame. Guess you'll be movin' on then, huh?"

"Nope."

She looked distressed. "Well, look, Mister. I can get your money back. You really oughta..."

"Cissy."

She sighed. "Yeah?"

"I am not here looking for work. I am here to do a job. Once the job is done, I'll leave."

She looked sick. "What job?"

"That doesn't concern you."

"Has it got anything to do with Red?"

I smiled and made it look reassuring. "You don't need to worry about Red."

I stepped into the front garden and collected a bundle of newspapers, including the *New York Times*, from the end of the drive, and brought them back inside. Cissy stared at me as she put a plate of pancakes and a pot of coffee on the table.

"What's that?"

I sat and started going through the classified ads. "Newspapers. You should try them. They're better than the TV."

She sat. I glanced at her. She still looked uncomfortable. "I don't get no news papers."

"I do. I ordered them yesterday."

"Sounds like you're planning on settling in." She didn't sound thrilled by the prospect. I smiled to myself as I opened the next paper. "Just a couple of days or three, Cissy. And I promise you'll be better off by the time I leave."

I found the ad in the *New York Times*, in the 'Lost and Found' section. It said, 'Kyle Rees, you have seen what you came to see. Now go home. Do your reading.'

I felt a hot pellet of anger in my belly, threw the paper on the table and sat drinking my coffee while Cissy buttered a pancake and chewed her lip. Kyle Rees, the loyal, obedient soldier, pawn of fate, father of the great hero, but destined never to be the hero himself. Born to serve, never to lead. I wondered sourly what that made Engels. Was he John Connor? I dismissed the thought, along with Marni, from my mind.

"So what does gossip say about where the Mexicans cross?"

She looked surprised. "Huh?"

"You don't read papers, but you must hear talk. What do people say? There some town 'round here where the Mexicans come in?"

She frowned. "You a cop?"

I laughed out loud, and I guess the way I laughed convinced her I wasn't a cop.

She smiled, then shrugged. "It's getting a lot harder, but they say a lot of people still get in through Abasse. That's in San Juan County." She hesitated. "Red's uncle is the sheriff down there."

"No kidding."

She nodded.

"I guess that's pretty handy for him."

She frowned. "What do you mean?"

I raised an eyebrow. "Do you know what Red does for a living, Cissy?"

"Well, what kind of a question is that? You been to his club last night!"

"Have *you* ever been to his club?"

"Uh-uh. Red don't like me goin' out. He says it's unladylike."

"I'll bet he does."

She stuffed a pancake in her mouth and tried to ignore me. I wasn't going to make it easy for her.

"His club is a bordello, and he sells cocaine."

Her face went pale. "That ain't none of my business..."

"The women get hurt. Does that surprise you, knowing

what you know about Red? Men go there and pay to beat up the women."

Her face went from very pale to a bright flush. "That ain't my problem. I don't know what you think I can do about it."

"Just because you ignore a problem, Cissy, doesn't mean it's not your problem. That little niggling and gnawing you're feeling in your conscience right now, that you're trying so hard to ignore? In time, that becomes hell. Next time he beats you black and blue, ask yourself how many sixteen-year-old girls has he done that to? Girls who came here looking for a better life, to help their brothers and sisters, and their mothers. And instead, they found themselves being beaten and raped, by the man you love, and share your bed with."

It was quite a speech, and I was wondering where the hell it came from. She was looking at me wide-eyed with her mouth half-open. I stood and took my plate and my cup into the kitchen and washed them up. When I came back, she said, "I want you to leave."

I smiled at her and shook my head. "I can't do that. But I'll tell you what, Cissy, if you have the balls to kick Red out, I'll leave too. How do I get to Abasse?"

There was real resentment in her eyes. Knights in shining armor were supposed to make your problems disappear. They were definitely not meant to make you face them and take responsibility for them.

"Tucson-Ajo Highway to Three Points, then turn south on the 286. Just follow it all the way to the border."

I stepped out into the brilliant morning sunshine,

climbed into my car, and headed west on Valencia till I came to the Ajo Highway. There I turned south, into the desert.

The Arizona desert is not like the Sahara or the Kalahari. It's not really a desert in that sense. Those are true deserts, dead places where, as far as the eye can see, there is only rock and dust, ochre, brown, red and black. Arizona is arid, but life is abundant, and southwest of Tucson, in the broad plain that stretches between Keystone Peak and the Baboquivari-Kitt Peak range, the pale dust produces a sparse woodland of sweet acacia, desert willow, palo verde and papago cacti. The heat, even in October, can be intense, and the brilliance of the early sun that morning was turning into a hot glare as it edged toward midday.

The smart thing would have been to close the windows, seal the car and turn on the AC. But how often do you get to drive through the Arizona desert in October? I opened all the windows and let the heat and the air blast me, and spent a couple of hours forgetting about Marni, my dead father, Cissy the eternal victim, and Red.

Red, whom I had decided to kill.

It was less than an hour's drive, but I took time to get off the blacktop and followed the dirt tracks to see where they led me. Mostly, by and by, they led me back to the main road.

I finally got to Abasse at noon. The first thing that struck me was that there was nobody there. It was like everybody had given up and gone home. Only, for a couple of hundred people, maybe less, this was home. There was a general store with two gas pumps outside, and a wooden bench with a parasol. And there was a handful of houses that all had iron bars on their windows and barbed wire fences around their yards. I parked and climbed out into the dusty heat.

Inside, the store was dark and cool. The guy behind the counter looked Mexican. His eyes told me he didn't like the fact that he didn't know me, but he was going to play nice just in case I shot him. It was that kind of place. I bought a pack of Pueblo cigarettes and as he was ringing up the sale, I said, "I need to arrange some border crossing. Who can I talk to?"

He pointed south. "The border is two minutes away, jus' follow the road."

I didn't move. I just kept staring at him with just enough of a smile to make him feel uncomfortable. He shook his head and spread his hands, appealing to me for understanding. "Please, *señor*, I don't know nothin'..."

I kept staring, but let the smile die. He sighed. "Maybe you can talk to *señor* Arana, but he don't like visitors, and if you tell him I sent you..."

I shook my head. "I am not going to tell him anything. I am just going to leave and you will never see me or hear from me again. Where can I find Arana?"

"*Señor* Arana and his friends, they are usually in the bar, go back, four hundred meters, you see a sign by the road, *Casa Coca*. Is maybe fifty meters down the track." He kind of winced. "But is kind of private. They don't like visitors."

I grinned. I hoped it was a friendly grin. "That's OK. They'll like me."

"Please, *señor*, don't tell them I told you..."

"Don't worry about it. Forget you ever saw me."

I stepped out into the heat and the glare and climbed into my car. I crawled back the way I'd come. Before long I came to a dirt track on my left with an old wooden sign that said, '*Casa Coca*'. They weren't shy, you had to say that for them. The sign looked old and dilapidated, and I figured it belonged to a time when they wanted to attract customers. I turned into the track and rolled along for forty yards till I came to a big adobe house on three floors. It had a broad, wooden porch with a vine growing over it, a door with a Mexican curtain and small windows that were designed not to let the light in, but to keep people out. There was a Jeep parked in the shade of a palo verde and I pulled in next to it.

What I saw when I stepped inside was not what I had expected. Maybe I'd expected to see Lee Van Cleef and Clint Eastwood smoking cheroots in the corner. What I saw was a comfortable bar that seemed better suited to Vegas than this remote border crossing. There were just two people there, and they were both staring at me, frowning.

One of them was the sheriff. He was in his fifties, lean, strong and tall. He had a gray crew cut and mean blue eyes. You could see the family resemblance with Red. He was wearing jeans and a khaki shirt, where he'd pinned his badge, sitting on a barstool with both hands loosely around a bottle of beer. Across the bar, there was a guy in a white shirt polishing a glass.

I did my best imitation of an amiable smile and ambled up to the bar.

"G'day. Any chance of a cold beer? I'm parched."

The barmen gave me the dead eye for a count of four and said, "I think you must have taken a wrong turning somewhere, friend. This is a private club."

The sheriff took things in hand and creased his concrete face with something he probably thought was a smile.

"Just keep going north. In less than an hour you'll come to Three Points. There's a restaurant right there on the crossroads."

"That's very civil of you, Sheriff. Problem is, I have a mighty thirst upon me right now." I looked at the guy behind the bar and said. "Gimme a cold beer there, will you, Sancho?" He went very still and I turned back to the sheriff. "While we're here having this friendly chat, maybe you can help me out."

His eyes went hard and cold. "Why don't you tell me who the hell you are and what you want, friend?"

"Well, that's exactly what I want. I want to be friends. I want to be friends with Mr. Arana. So I thought I'd drop in and say hello. And to break the ice, I thought I'd sell him some information."

"You got exactly five seconds to turn around and get the hell out of here, mister..."

"I don't think that would be smart, Sheriff. And to be honest, I don't know if I should be talking to you, or Sancho over here." I turned to look at the guy in the white shirt. "What do you say, Sancho?"

"I say the next time you call me Sancho I'm gonna cut your fuckin' throat."

"Can he threaten me like that, Sheriff? Is that allowed? Are my five seconds up?" I turned back to the guy behind the bar. "Where is my beer, Sancho?"

I didn't wait for a reaction. I put the Sig to the sheriff's eye and said, "It's cocked and the safety's off, Sheriff. I would advise you not to move." I grinned at Sancho. "Now are you going to give me a fucking beer or do I have to come around there and beat one out of you?"

As I said it, I smashed the butt of the Sig into the sheriff's ear and knocked him off his perch on the barstool. He crashed to the floor in a mess and lay groaning holding his head. My guess was he felt real sick and had a bad headache. Sancho reached in the fridge for a beer. I climbed on the stool and kept talking.

"Now, my guess is that this guy wears the badge, but you are the man to talk to. Am I right?"

"*Señor* Arana is at the casino. He ain't gonna waste time talkin' to a punk like you. What the fuck do you want?"

"I already told you. I have information that he needs and I am willing to sell. And that is going to be the beginning of a long and beautiful relationship."

He made a face of contempt. "What information? You full of shit."

I took a long pull on the beer, smacked my lips and sighed. "Friend, in thirty seconds I am going to walk out of here. After that, what you do is your business. But I can tell you this: I, personally, would not want to be the one who has to explain to Arana why I chose *not* to pass on the information that could have avoided what's going to happen next."

He frowned hard and looked real worried.

"Huh? What's gonna happen next?"

I leaned forward and leered at him. "That is for sale, Sancho." I pointed the automatic between his eyes. "I'll be back here tomorrow night. If Arana isn't here, I'm going to want to know why."

On the floor the sheriff was dragging himself into a sitting position. I climbed off the stool and walked back out into the glaring sun and the heat. As I pulled out of the dirt track onto the 286, I wondered vaguely to myself what the hell I was doing, and why I was getting involved in Cissy's problems. I settled back and started cruising north, toward Three Points. I told myself I was killing time until I got some action from Marni. But I knew I was kidding myself. I knew it went deeper than that.

SIX

I DROVE BACK INTO TUCSON, STOPPED FOR A hamburger at Chilli's Grill, and sat over a coffee and a whiskey staring blindly at the receiver for the tracking device I'd put under Marni's car. I was wondering what the hell I was going to do next. I was restless, angry and unfocused. It was bad, and I knew it was bad.

I sat like that until the sun started making long shadows across the concrete parking lot outside. Then I had another coffee and another whiskey. I still hadn't reached any kind of decision when the tracker bleeped and started to move.

I paid up and climbed back in the car. I put the tracker on the dash and followed the bleep to the Park Place Shopping Mall, on East Broadway Boulevard. I didn't go in. Instead I accelerated past and threw a right onto South Prudence Road, which took me all the way to Carson Corner. I pulled in to Tamara Drive and parked fifty yards from her house, as the sun went down.

I walked up like I owned the place, picked the lock in

fifteen seconds, stepped inside and closed the door behind me. I was in a spacious, open-plan living room-diner with broad glass doors onto a back garden with a pool. Houses without pools are the exception in Tucson. The room was sparsely furnished in neutral colors. There were no photographs or pictures, or any kind of ornament. There was nothing that said that Marni lived here. In spite of the heat outside, it felt cold.

I wanted to look around and explore, but I knew my time was limited and she would soon be on her way back. I had to act fast. I put the first bug under her coffee table. It was essentially a voice-activated, miniaturized cell-phone in the form of a chip that was pre-dialed into my laptop. If anybody started talking, it would activate and leave whatever it heard in a file on my hard drive. It was clever stuff.

I climbed the stairs to the top floor. There were two bedrooms and a bathroom. One bedroom was unused and the bed was just a bare mattress, still wrapped in plastic. The other was clearly hers. I left a second bug under her bedside table, hoping with a sour twist that it never got activated.

I opened her wardrobe. There were very few clothes, but I found a rucksack and a pair of leather boots. I placed one tracker in the rucksack and another in her right boot. They worked on a GPS system. When she left, wherever she went, I'd be able to find her.

I stood a moment in the doorway, looking at the room and the tousled quilt on the bed. I had a strange sense of loss. I should not be spying on her, I should be a part of this room, of her life. Which was absurd, because I had told her in London, five years back, that there could never be anything between us. She could never be a part of the sick life I had created for myself. So why now? Why this sense of loss now?

Something on her bedside table caught my eye. It was a passport, an ID card and a driver's license. I picked them up and examined them. The photographs were of her, but the name was Mandy Gillan. The quality was good, almost perfect. I wondered how she'd got hold of them. The Marni I knew would not have had access to the kind of people who make near perfect fake IDs. Did I know her? Did I know her at all?

The tracker in my pocket told me she was on the move again. I checked and saw she was headed back toward home. No time for questions now. No time for soul searching.

I ran down the stairs, stepped out into the darkening evening and walked to my car. I didn't wait for her to arrive. I didn't want to see if she was alone. If Engels was with her, right then I didn't want to know that.

On the way back to Cissy's I stopped at a supermarket and bought two bottles of wine, one red and one white. They were both good and both were damned expensive. I was a rich man now, and I could afford it; and besides, there was a growing, wild anger inside me that I couldn't explain —or at least I didn't want to explain—and all I kept telling myself was that I didn't give a good goddamn about anything. I didn't give a damn that Red and Chetan were selling women like Lucia to perverts so that they could beat them up; I didn't give a damn that Red was beating up and raping Cissy, and I didn't give a damn that she believed she loved him. And I sure as hell didn't give a damn that Marni was teaming up with Engels, taking him into her confidence, while she was telling me to 'go home' and 'do my reading'.

When I got back to the bed and breakfast, it was dark and the stars were brilliant and cold overhead. I rang on the bell and Cissy opened almost immediately, like she'd been waiting. She'd put makeup on, maybe to conceal her bruises. The swelling on her eye had gone down. I smiled at her and she smiled back, a little nervous. I held up the bottles.

"A peace offering. I hope you like wine."

"You shouldn't have. There was no need. I shouldn'a said the things I said."

I handed her the white. "That one could go in the freezer for half an hour." She took it and as she put it in the fridge, I started rummaging in the cutlery drawer for a corkscrew. "It's your house, Cissy. You have a right to kick me out if you want to."

I found what I was searching for and straightened to look at her. "I'll be gone in a couple of days anyway, so if you can wait I'd appreciate it. But I was wrong, and I apologize." I shrugged. "I was kind of mad."

She listened to me in silence. As I started to uncork the bottle, she said, "I wasn't sure when you'd be back. I ain't cooked anything."

"That's OK. We can have a drink before supper."

"I don't usually drink much."

I held her eye a moment and saw her cheeks color. "Will you make an exception tonight?"

"I suppose a glass of wine won't do any harm."

"Harm? It'll do you good."

She giggled. "I hope Red don't turn up!"

"If he does, we'll offer him a glass too."

Her eyes opened in fake alarm. "Oh, Lord!"

"You got some music?"

"Well sure!"

She put on some country music and I started peeling potatoes. I put on a kind of generic southern accent and said, "When y'all done there, y'all could git me a beer."

She squealed with laughter, like I'd said something hilarious. It was easy to make her laugh, and that made her easy to have around. It also made it easy to forget all the things I didn't want to remember. She poured me a beer and I poured her a glass of cold white wine, and we ended up dancing while the French fries cooked in the deep fryer. We laughed a lot at stupid things—because she laughed at anything I said, and I laughed at the way she laughed. It was good.

After dinner, we sat on the sofa and watched a movie on TV. I put my arm around her and after ten minutes, she rested her head on my shoulder. It was comfortable. It was a nice feeling, and for an hour or two I pretended to myself that it was normal; that I could have this, like other men had.

Before the end of the movie, she was snoring quietly, and I stroked her hair and kissed the top of her head. When the film was over, I picked her up and carried her upstairs. I laid her on her bed and stood for a long moment wondering what to do. In the end, I undressed her and put her under the covers. Then I went down, washed up and went to my room, where I lay and stared at the ceiling, fighting the unexpressed rage I had inside me.

Half an hour passed and there was a soft tap at my door. My fingers closed instinctively on my Sig under the pillow.

"Yeah?"

The door opened and Cissy stepped in. "Do you mind?"

"Of course not. What is it?"

She came over and sat on the bed. "You are *such* a gentle-man. You know how few men would do what you just done?"

I smiled. "Shucks, Ma'am, it's jist the way I was raised."

"Stop it! Now move over an' let me show you how we do things, Arizona style."

I made room for her, smiled, and sank gratefully into the warmth of her arms.

SEVEN

I woke up late. The morning sun was laying twisted oblongs of light across the bed, and an early breeze was moving the curtains. Cissy was up. I could hear her downstairs. She had the radio playing country classics, and she was singing along. For a moment, I felt a stab of guilt that I couldn't put into words. I rose and went to stare at myself in the bathroom mirror. Had I led Cissy to believe there could be something, that we were going somewhere?

And then I wondered, why not? Why could other men have a home and a family and a beautiful wife, but not me?

Because I was a killer. It was what I was born and trained to be. And Cissy, like Marni, deserved better than what I was, better than I could ever be.

I shaved, then stood under the hot jets of the shower, turned them to ice cold and felt better. As I toweled myself dry, I could see Sergeant Bradley in my mind, the light from the camp fire making his eyes diabolical under the night sky of the desert. His deep, New Zealand voice was oddly reassuring in the presence of imminent death.

"Men like you and me, Lacklan, we shouldn't go soul-searching," He had leered like a ghastly, Antipodean gnome, "I mean, who the fuck would want to find what *we* have in our souls?"

He wasn't wrong.

I dressed and went downstairs. Cissy beamed at me from the kitchen. The swelling over her eye was almost gone, and she'd put plenty of makeup over her bruises. She came and kissed me, like a wife.

"I was just comin' up to call you, sleepy head."

I ignored my conscience, I kissed her back and went along with the game. It was nice to pretend. It couldn't last. But while it lasted, I planned to enjoy it.

We had chit-chat over breakfast, discussed what she had to get at the store and what I wanted for supper. As she cleared the table, she said, "I'll get all the big stuff on the weekend. Maybe you can give me a hand..."

She froze over the sink, realizing what she'd said. The weekend meant Saturday. Saturday meant Red. And in any case, by then I would probably be gone. I stood and went to her. I turned her around to face me and she forced a smile, like nothing was happening.

I said, "Trust me. It's going to be OK."

For a fraction of a second I saw Bradley's face, smeared with boot polish, staring at me in the dark. "Hey, trust me. It's going to be all right..." That night thirty men had died. None of them was SAS. We had done the killing. So Bradley had been right. Everything was all right.

She blinked and smiled. "Would you look at me, standing around like I got all day!"

She grabbed her purse and her keys. Then she stopped and pointed at the breakfast bar. "You're gonna need some keys. I left a set on the bar for you."

I watched her drive away and went to get my laptop.

There were no audio files. Marni had not spoken to anybody last night. She hadn't even watched TV or listened to music. I knew what she'd done. She had read, and written.

The rest of the day passed slowly. Her tracker was silent and she didn't talk. I drove over to Carson Corner three times. Her car was still in the drive. The impulse to go in there and confront her, find out what the hell she was doing and why she was cutting me out, became almost irresistible, but I fought it and waited. Was it wise patience? Or was it stupid pride?

Finally, as the sun slipped toward the hills in the west and the air started to turn to grainy dusk, I went up to my room, cleaned and oiled the Sig and spent five minutes sharpening the two sides of the blade on my Fairbairne & Sykes. When it was sharp enough to split a floating hair, I slipped it into my boot. I was taking the Sig to cover my bases, but I was pretty sure I wasn't going to need to use it.

The fighting knife was a whole different story. Messrs Fairbairn & Sykes would drink deep that night.

It was dark by the time I got to the *Casa Coca*. As I pulled down the drive, I was pleased to see half a dozen trucks, a couple of Audis and a Cadillac, all parked outside. The trip would not be wasted. I climbed out of the car and slammed the door loud enough to be heard. Desert nights are cold, and I could see the clouds of condensation running like scared ghosts from my mouth, dissipating in the dark. I stood a moment, looking up at the sky. Night skies in Arizona are one of the most beautiful sights on this planet. It was not a bad place, or a bad way, to die.

I looked over at the building. There was a soft light burning under the wooden veranda, and there was a big guy leaning in the doorway smoking a cigarette and watching me.

I walked across the dirt, stepped onto the porch and stood in front of him. I'm over six foot tall, but he was looking down at me.

"I'm here to see Arana. Move."

He didn't take the cigarette out of his mouth to speak, so it wagged on his lip and small clouds of ash trailed down onto his gray shirt.

"Fock you."

Everything was against him. I'd had a frustrating day. I was feeling impatient. I was keen to see Arana. And, most of all, I was convinced that there are already too many guys like this in the world.

However big a guy is, if he has a big gut and you punch down onto it, the combined weight of his belly and your punch will drag down on his diaphragm, wind him and, sometimes, even paralyze his heart. I put all of my two hundred and twenty pounds into the punch. His eyes bulged and he went a pasty gray color as he leaned forward, gaping his ugly mouth and wheezing for air. His suffering didn't last long. I slipped my knife from my boot and rammed into his fifth intercostal, right up close to his sternum, and felt him shudder as his heart went into spasm. I let him slip to the floor and stepped over him to open the door.

I went in, wiping the blade on my jeans, and let the door swing closed behind me. At a quick estimate, I figured there were two dozen guys there, and maybe half that many women. Most of the guys were of the big, bad, and stupid variety. There were a couple of suits and there was one I knew straight away was Arana. His suit was expensive, Italian and vulgar. He had enough gold on him to sink a tanker, and you could tell by his eyes that he made up in psychotic sadism for everything he lacked in intelligence.

All of this I saw as the voices in the room fell silent. I made a point of ignoring Arana and looking at every other face in the room. They all stared back at me. The Mexican music they were playing on the hi-fi sounded suddenly kind of embarrassed, and too loud.

"Which one of you is Arana? I need to talk to him."

I slipped my knife back in my boot and waited. The suit sitting next to Arana stood and shouted, "*Quien coño es el pendejo este? Donde esta Dixon?*" Which translates roughly to, who the fuck is this guy and where is Dixon?

"Dixon is dead. And I'm the guy who's going to save your ass. Are you Arana?"

He scowled at me and shouted at the four guys at the table nearest. He was nothing if not predictable.

"*Atrápenlo ya, cojones! A que esperan?*"

Get him. What the hell are you waiting for? I smiled at the guys as they scrambled to their feet. I could have shot each one of them in those four long seconds, but I had a point to make, so I let them come.

The biggest came first, with bulging yellow eyes and

breath that stank of onions and cigarettes. His brains were as rudimentary as his technique. He lunged at me with both hands. I don't know what he planned to do once he had me. He probably didn't know himself. I didn't really care. I rammed the middle knuckles of my left hand into his windpipe as I pulled my knife back out from my boot. Then I pushed him aside to choke to death on the floor while the other three rushed me.

The thing when you're being rushed by more than two guys, is to always strike at the one on your far right. That forces them to turn left, and into each other. That was what I did then. I stepped to my right. The nearest guy went for me, and I took his left wrist in my left hand as he reached for my collar. With a quick slash, I severed the tendons in his armpit. He didn't feel it at first. But when he saw the blood spurting out and realized he couldn't move his arm, he started screaming over the Mexican music. That much took all of two seconds.

The other two tried to get to me, but their screaming pal was in the way. I stepped behind him and shoved him hard into their path with my boot. The farthest, a blond guy with a pencil mustache, was shouting at him to get out of the way as blood sprayed over his face and his shirt. The nearest one gritted his teeth and thrust at me with a blade he'd pulled from his jacket. He was off-balance because of trying to get around his screaming buddy, and because his technique sucked. I took his wrist and deflected his thrust across his body so that he stumbled toward me, onto my blade. I was already moving toward the big blond as I cut up into number three's solar plexus, and let him fall, jumping and quivering, to the floor.

I looked hard into the blond's eyes and said, "Don't!" He hesitated just long enough for me to slice across his throat. His brain bled out in a couple of seconds. His eyes rolled up and he dropped. The guy with the severed tendons had gone down and was slipping into coma. His legs kept twitching. The floor was awash with blood. The whole thing had happened in less than ten seconds. If you count out ten seconds in your mind, it's a long time when you're killing people.

I wiped the blade on my jeans for the second time and looked at the suit. I said, "Sit down."

He did. Then I looked at Arana, whose face was wearing a 'what the fuck' expression. I pointed at him with my knife, just to let him know there were no boundaries here. "You ready to stop playing compare dicks and start talking? Or do I have to kill some of your suits, too?" I waited. He didn't say anything. I went on, "All I want is to sell you some information you need to know."

The Mexican band wailed on. There was a moment of complete stillness. I could feel the Sig p226 hard against my back. I was pretty sure of what would happen next, but if he got the wrong look in his eye, I'd shoot the suit and blow Arana's knee in half before his apes had time to say *"Ayayay!"*

Luckily for him, he did what he had to do. His eyes turned sullen and he snarled at his right-hand man, "Get this fockin' mess cleaned up, Juan, what you fockin' waiting for?" To me he said, "Sit down, wha's this fantastic information you have for me?"

Juan the Suit got up and started shouting at people. Crying girls brought mops from the kitchen, and a couple of guys got hold of some bed sheets and big black garbage sacks. By gradual degrees, the four things that had, only a few minutes earlier, been people, were dragged out into the desert night, to be buried, eaten, and forgotten. That was the path they had chosen, and that was where that path led. Maybe that was where my path led too. I didn't know, and right then I didn't care.

EIGHT

I SAT WITH MY BACK TO THE WALL, PULLED A Pueblo from my pack and told the waitress, "Irish, no ice." I lit up with my battered, brass Zippo, breathed the smoke deep into my lungs and studied his face.

"You think you have coke and prostitution sewn up in this area."

He shrugged. "So what?"

"You haven't."

The waitress brought my drink. She had tears in her eyes and her hands were shaking. She couldn't have been more than seventeen.

"So tell me. Who else is runnin' blow and *putas*?"

I gave a laugh that was about as amused as a gay bishop at a stag night. "What am I now, your new best friend? Have I got 'stupid' written across my forehead? Who do I have to fucking kill around here for you to take me seriously? You want me to kill fucking Juan over there? Should I kill Juan?"

It was a good performance. It scared the bejaysus out of

Juan, who dropped one of the corpses' legs and stared from me to Arana and back again in alarm.

Arana raised his hands and looked irritated. "Take it easy! *Cojones!* You don't need to kill nobody else! What's your price?"

"Five thousand bucks, and..." I pointed at the last of the bodies being dragged out through the door. "Looks like you have a vacancy. I want a job. I plan on sticking around for a while."

He looked both skeptical and uncomfortable. "You want a job, with me?"

I raised an eyebrow at him. "Think about it, Arana. If I plan to report for duty tomorrow morning, that has to mean my information is good, right?" His eyebrow twitched. I moved right on before he could think it through. "Plus, I just killed five of your men, and instead of getting killed myself, I'm sitting here drinking whiskey with you. How many men do you know who can pull that off? I'll eliminate your competition and double your income before the end of the month. I am useful to you, and you know it."

He scowled at me. Then, predictably, he started laughing. "OK, *amigo!*" He slapped me on the shoulder and turned to Juan. "Juanito! Go to the safe. Bring five grand for our new Marketing Manager! *Carmencita! Traiga tequila!*"

Carmencita, looking a little less scared, brought a bottle of tequila, a handful of shot glasses, a dish of lemon and a pot of salt. Arana watched me watching her as she set them down on the table. "You like her, *amigo*? She is for you. Now, tell me, what is this information?"

I sipped my whiskey and studied his face. I waited till Juan came hurrying back out with a large manila envelope.

He gave it to Arana who opened it and showed me the contents. It looked like five thousand dollars in large bills. I said, "You have a Judas among your disciples."

He scowled. "A Judas?"

"Yeah. Somebody I figure you pay a lot of money to, to keep things sweet. He's helping to set up an operation competing directly with you."

"Who is this son of a bitch?"

"The sheriff of San Juan County. He's helping his nephew, Red, to set up a club in Tucson. They're buying crack and girls down in Mexico and selling them up here. I'm guessing you didn't know about that operation. Hand over the money, pal. Let's stay friends."

His face flushed and he screamed for a bit in Spanish, about the sheriff being a son of the great whore, and all the things he was going to do to various parts of his anatomy. I reached over, took the money and put it in my jacket pocket. He watched me do it with staring eyes.

"How you know this?"

"That's none of your goddamn business, Arana. Tomorrow night he's going to be at his club at eight PM. Camino del Oeste, where it makes the corner, on the edge of the desert. He'll have a shipment that he brought from his supplier south of the border. Don't go. Send your four best men with automatic weapons. I'll be there. We'll wipe out the gang, collect the dope and bring you Red. You interrogate him, find out who his supplier is, and I'll wipe him out too. Deal?"

He didn't like the way I was talking to him, but he liked the plan. After a moment he leered. "OK, deal."

I knocked back the whiskey and stood. Arana looked

disappointed. Maybe he hoped we'd hang out and be pals. I signaled to Carmencita. "Get your bag, sweetheart. We're going home." To Arana I said, "Give me a cell where I can contact you."

He spread his hands. "What's your hurry, *gringo*? You don't like my tequila?"

I didn't smile. "When Red is lying out in the desert feeding the buzzards, and his club is being hosed down by the fire department, then I'll drink tequila with you. Tonight I'm going to sleep. And tomorrow I am going to solve your problem."

Carmencita was standing with her bag looking down at Arana. Her legs were shaking. She said, "*Que hago, Jefe?*"

She was asking him what to do. I gave him a look that said he shouldn't upset me and he snarled, "*Vaya con el. Hágale feliz.*"

He'd told her to go with me and make me happy. I jerked my head toward the door and she moved that way. I turned back to Arana and he handed me a card. I took it and said, "I'll see you tomorrow night, about twelve or one." I gave the shadow of a smile. "Then we'll drink tequila and party."

He nodded. Right then we both knew that his plan was to kill me tomorrow. He knew I was much too dangerous for his peace of mind. But what he didn't know was that by tomorrow things would be looking very different.

Outside, the desert air was icy. I got into the car and Carmencita climbed in beside me. The doors slammed, shutting out the cold. She put her hands between her knees and stared down at them, as though if she focused hard enough she could make me and the nightmare I represented go away.

The engine roared, the hazy funnels of the headlamps

broke into the darkness, and the reverse gear whined as I pulled back up the track and onto the road. I stopped, put it in drive, and then we were sliding forward through the night, with the twisted trees springing out like shocks in a nightmare, only to fade away again behind us, in the blackness of the desert. Over in the east, the first sliver of the moon was rising over the hills. We drove on in silence for about ten minutes. Then I said to her, "Carmencita, do you speak English?"

She nodded at her hands. "Yes."

"I want you to understand something. The decisions you make tonight—the choices you make—will determine what happens to you and your family for the rest of your life. Do you understand that?"

She nodded again, harder. "Yes, *señor*, I will do anything you want. Please don't hurt me or my family."

I sighed. "No, Carmencita. I am not here to hurt you or your family. I am here to help you. You have an opportunity tonight. A lucky break. I want you to do the right thing." I glanced at her and asked again. "Do you understand?"

She was watching me. The dim light from the dash touched the planes of her face, making her look beautiful but ghostly. She said simply, "No..."

"I am not a good man, but I am not a monster and I do not traffic in drugs or human beings. I can't explain to you why I am here tonight. It's too complicated. But I can tell you that I am not here to hurt you, and if you trust me, I will help you."

The only answer she could give was to swallow and keep watching me. I reached in my jacket and pulled out the manila envelope with the money in it. I handed it to her.

"Take it. I don't need it and I don't want it."

She hesitated a moment, then took the money.

"Why? What do you want from me?"

Up ahead I could see the glow of Three Points. I tried to think of a way I could explain it so she would understand. I couldn't.

"Nothing," I said, "I don't want anything from you. All I want is for you to make a couple of smart decisions tonight."

"What kind of decisions?"

"Have you got family back home?"

"My mother and my brother."

"I am going to give you an address near Boston. It's my house. I want you to go there. I'll phone ahead. There will be people there to take care of you and sort out your papers. If you want to go back home, you can. If you want to stay, I'll give you a job."

She narrowed her eyes and shook her head. "*Why?* Nobody does this for nothing..."

I felt suddenly defeated. "Maybe for that very reason, Carmencita. Because nobody ever does anything for nothing. Maybe it's time we did."

After a moment, I phoned Kenny. I put it on speaker and set it on the jack, so she could hear our conversation. It rang a few times, then Kenny spoke, sounding sleepy.

"Mr. Walker, sir..."

"Kenny, I'm sorry to wake you up. It's a bit of an emergency. Everything OK back home?"

"Everything is fine, sir. What can I do for you?"

"I have a friend here who needs some help. Her name is Carmen, or Carmencita. I'm putting her on the next flight to Boston. I'd like you to meet her at the airport. We'll put her up for a few days till she decides what she wants to do. Make her feel at home. She's had a bad time."

"Of course, sir. Just send me the details when you have the ticket."

"Thanks, Kenny. Good night."

We didn't talk again until we got to the airport. It was cavernous and hollow and lonely at that time of night. We walked with echoing steps to the American Airlines desk and I got her a ticket. Her flight was at five-fifty in the morning, which gave her about five hours to sleep.

I walked her to the departure gates. There she stopped and squinted at me, like I was some kind of equation that didn't work out. She shrugged and shook her head in that way Latinas do.

"What are you, some kind of weird religious freak?"

"No. And you can walk away any time you like. Keep the money. I'm just a guy who is sick of all the ugliness, and I figure if I want the world to be a better place, then maybe I have to start with me. I'm not out to help people. You just happened to cross my path. It was your lucky day. Don't pay me back. Like the movie, pay it forward."

She nodded a few times, like she was trying to believe me but having trouble. Finally she turned, without saying anything, and walked away into the departure lounge.

I went back across the big hall, listening to the echoes of my feet. Every damn step you take in life has an infinite number of echoes, I told myself. And they all sound empty and cold and hollow.

Outside, under the icy Arizona stars, I sat on the hood of my rental car and lit up a Pueblo with my battered old

Zippo. I breathed the smoke down deep, put Carmencita out of my mind and thought about what I was going to do next.

Next, I was going to cause mayhem and murder.

THE MOON WAS high enough to throw a shroud of turquoise light over the world. And the streets were quiet enough to be able to hear all the sounds of the desert, the cries and the howls and the baying of the predators. The victims in nature are mostly silent. It's only human victims that make a noise.

I let myself in the house and closed the door silently behind me. It was still and dark. I climbed the stairs and stopped on the landing. The door to my room was closed. Hers was open a couple of inches. I hesitated. I knew what I should do. I should go into my room. I should not get any closer to her. I should not let her get any closer to me. But I am not perfect. If there is one thing I am not, it's perfect. And a person gets tired of being alone. I stepped into her room and closed the door. I heard her voice, sleepy and warm.

"Lacklan, honey? Is that you?"

I smiled. What the hell. Life is too short to turn away the good stuff.

NINE

W HEN I GOT UP FROM HER BED AND WENT OUT TO run, it was still dark. The moon was setting in the east, but the predators had gone silent. I ran hard. The icy air tore at my throat and my breath and my feet sounded loud in the darkness. I ran for half an hour, then trained hard, feeling my muscles strain, enjoying the pain and the adrenaline, trying to silence my mind.

I had a choice, and I did not want to think about it. I kicked and punched the air, controlling my breathing, focusing my mind on each death blow, remembering the feeling of breaking bones, of cracking ribs, of all the people I had maimed and killed over the years.

I had got in too deep. That was the way I had lived my whole life: in too deep.

But I had come here for Marni, to find out what she was doing, to protect her, as my father had asked me to do. Now, instead, I was driving myself deeper into a potentially lethal situation that did not concern me, that had nothing to do with me.

I kept asking myself what the hell I was playing at, and the only answer I could get was the image of Red's face, sneering at me and at Cissy, and Arana's face, sneering at me and at Carmencita. And the urge to destroy them was too strong. It was overwhelming. It was not a desire, it was a compulsion. It was a need.

Blindly, I delivered six punches in less than a second, and bellowed a *kiai* that echoed among the hills.

As it died away, I realized that the sun was rising. I had been training for an hour. I returned to Cissy's house at a slow, loose run, allowing the blood to flow through my muscles and ease the tension. As I ran, I told myself it was time to talk to Marni; time to cut the crap and stop playing games. Either she dealt me in or I was out. She did not get to play me any longer.

When I let myself in, Cissy was in the kitchen making breakfast. She came to the door to give me a kiss. Her cheerfulness was strained.

"Five minutes, big boy."

I went up to shower.

When I got down, she'd made a breakfast that was big enough for a main meal. Bacon, fried bananas, waffles, maple syrup. It was fine because I was hungry, but I knew it meant something. She laughed when she saw my face.

"I figured you burned so much energy last night and this morning..."

I smiled, sat and started eating. She sat opposite. I eyed her a moment and swallowed.

"It's Friday."

She became serious. "I know."

"You're wondering what's going to happen. What I'm going to do."

She nodded. "It's fine. I know I started it. I came to your room. You was a perfect gentleman…"

"I'm not going to let him hurt you again."

She tried to read my face, what that meant. "How…?"

"My life is a mess, Cissy. You don't want to be involved with me. I'm a killer. That's what I do. I'd like to be a better person, but it's too late for that. I can't change what I am or what I've become."

She gave a small frown.

"A killer…?"

I smiled. "I'm not a hit man, Cissy. It's complicated. Too complicated to explain, and in any case it's best you don't know. But I can't give you the kind of life that you deserve…" I paused, hesitated, unsure whether to say it, whether it was honest. "…Even though I would like to. But I can promise you one thing. Red is never going to hurt you again. Not tomorrow, not ever."

She swallowed. "Are you going to hurt him? Are you going to kill him…?"

I held her eye for a long moment. "Are you sure you want to know?"

She shook her head. "No."

I climbed the stairs to my room and switched on the laptop. There was an audio file from the night before. I opened it.

At first it was hard to make out the voices. It was Marni and a man. I figured they were over by the door, away from the table. I heard the door close and the quality improved. Marni said, "You want a drink?"

A man's voice, it sounded like Engels: "Yeah, what have you got?"

"Not much, beer."

He laughed. "OK, I'll have a beer."

The sound of the fridge opening and closing. Some indistinct movement. Then Engels, "Cheers. You got a glass...?"

A snort from Marni, then silence while she went for a glass. I sighed, feeling strangely anxious and angry without knowing why. Then Marni's voice said, "So, any news?"

"Yeah, I told you I have some contacts in Washington. I spoke to them and heard back yesterday. There is a senator. I can't tell you his name yet, but he is willing to talk to us."

"What do we know about him?"

"He's one of the good guys. He has a long track record of fighting in the environmental corner, even at the expense of his own financial benefit. He has lobbied on behalf of conservation and environmental protection against large corporations and the petrochemical industry. He is squeaky clean."

"What's his background? Where does his money come from?" I nodded. That was the right question to be asking.

"I'm coming to that. For the last five years, he has been campaigning quietly, behind the scenes, to get Congress to look at the issue of overpopulation and climate change as the biggest threats facing humanity in this century. He is our man."

There was silence for a couple of beats. Then she asked again, "Where does his money come from?"

Engels' voice again, a little strained. "It's old money. His family came over from Wiltshire, in England, in the seventeenth century, escaping from Cromwell. They brought their fortune with them."

She was quiet for a long time, then asked, "You trust him?"

"I do, yeah."

"What's his idea?"

A loud sigh from Engels. "He has the connections in Congress and in the media. He knows who we can trust and who we can't. You know as well as I do that the media is controlled by four or five major interests, what we don't know is which of those interests is in bed with this Omega organization. It may be all of them for all we know. He will be able to guide us. We need him as an ally."

All the hair on the back of my neck bristled. I could smell a trap and even though the conversation had happened almost twelve hours earlier, my mind was screaming at Marni not to trust him. *Why the hell had she cut me out?*

She was saying, "When does he want to meet?"

"Tomorrow evening."

I was on my feet, swearing violently, *"Shit! Shit! Shit!"* I grabbed the pants I'd been wearing the night before, searching through the pockets, grabbed my jacket from the back of the door, found the tracker and stared at the screen. There had been no movement. She was still in the house. I ran, grabbing my Sig and jamming it in my waistband, taking the stairs three at a time.

I vaguely heard Cissy's voice calling after me as I wrenched open the car door. The tires squealed as I pulled away. I cursed myself for not bringing the Zombie as I screeched onto Camino de La Tierra, speeding north toward Valencia Road. I cursed myself for going against my instincts and trying to play smart, give her space. I double-cursed myself for not confronting her head-on.

The lights were red at Valencia, so I hit the gas, accelerated over the sidewalk and cut the corner across a patch of dirt. Horns blared at me but I didn't give a damn and floored the pedal west for twelve miles, to Kolb Road, cursing myself every inch of the way for a damned fool, pounding the wheel with my fist. What the hell had got into me? What the hell had possessed me to get involved in Cissy's damn fool relationship with Red? Pissing around like some damn jackass with Arana and Carmencita, while Marni was slipping through my fingers!

Sergeant Bradley's ugly face loomed large in my mind, *"It's a bloody dereliction of duty!"*

I threw the car left onto Kolb, corrected some violent under steer and hit sixty going north for three miles. Then I screamed right onto Stella and left onto Cordova, and skidded to a stop, blocking her drive on Brooks. Her gray Ford Focus was still there. I scrambled from the car and ran to the door, still swearing at myself. I should have been here last night. I should have been sitting on the house. More than that, I should have been a part of the damned conversation!

Why had she cut me out? *Why? Why? Why?*

I hammered on the door and rang the bell. There was no reply, no sound. I reached in my pocket and pulled out my lock picks. In fifteen seconds, I was in.

"Marni! It's me, Lacklan!"

The silence was an empty silence. I knew as I stood by

the door that she was gone. I ran up the stairs and wrenched open the wardrobe. Her rucksack and her boots were still there. Obviously she had gone with Engels in his car.

"*Fuck!*"

I went to the bedside table. The fake ID was gone. I kept hearing Sergeant Bradley's voice, his raw Kiwi rasp, "*Fuckin' dereliction of duty!*"

Duty. Loyalty. Fidelity.

A rage that was less than human welled up in my gut, a rage against myself, but a rage also against the whole damned human race. And a rage against Marni, the one, the only person I had ever trusted.

Duty is born of loyalty. And loyalty is a two-way damned street. I went down to the kitchen and found the keys to her car in the fruit bowl. I also found a spare set of house keys in a kitchen drawer. I put them in my pocket, then I went outside, opened the hood of the Focus and removed the sparkplug wires.

After that, I locked up the house and drove at a more sedate pace to the School of Natural Resources. Five minutes on the university website told me where Engels had his office, and I walked there feeling kind of sick.

His secretary managed to combine friendliness, impatience and surprise all into a single smile as I stepped in to her domain. She didn't say anything, like she was waiting to find out if she actually needed to talk to me. Maybe she didn't talk to anyone below a PhD. I tried to smile like a PhD and said, "I'd like to talk to Professor Engels. Is he in?"

I knew he wasn't, but I was hoping she'd tell me where he was. She didn't.

"Have you an appointment?"

"No, but it's kind of urgent." I repeated the question, "Is he in?"

"I'm afraid not. He's out of town for a couple of days."

"A couple of days?" I felt a hot twist in my gut. "Can you tell me where he's gone?"

She smiled like I was sweet but kind of sad. "I'm afraid not."

"As I said, it is urgent. Is there any way I can contact him?"

"I am sure it is, but I am just not in a position to hand out his contact details to anyone who turns up claiming to have an urgent need..." The smile she gave me was not warm. "I can try and get a message to him, if you'd like."

She raised an eyebrow, like she already knew I was going to say no.

I smiled back at her with dead eyes. "Thanks, I don't need you to talk to him. I need to talk to him. You understand the difference?"

"I can't help you..."

But I was already on my way down the stairs as she answered. I was wasting her time, and she was wasting mine.

I wasted a few more minutes sitting in the car, smoking and swearing at myself. I had let her slip through my fingers in the most negligent, amateur way. But self-recrimination would not fix anything. I had left myself just one option. I had to wait for her to get back. But when she did, I would not let her get away again.

I would be there, at her house, waiting for her.

TEN

I DROVE BACK TO THE BED AND BREAKFAST TELLING myself I had to get back on track. I had to disengage from Cissy, Red and Arana. I had made a mistake in getting involved, now I had to cut my losses and get out. I had thought I could bring down Arana and Red's operations as a sideline while watching Marni with one eye. It was my stupid arrogance I believed I could do anything—with a gun and a knife and a pack of C4, I was invincible. I had been arrogant and rash, and wasn't that exactly what my father had always complained about in me? Wasn't that exactly what he had tried to tell me in Colorado, at Rho's ranch, before Marni shot him?

Now I had to make it right. I'd move out of Cissy's and into Marni's house, and wait for her there. I felt a bitter twist in my gut. It was the best thing for Cissy anyway. The last thing she needed in her life after Red was me.

Red.

I pulled up outside her house and let myself in with the

key she'd given me. I knew straight away that things were not going to work out as I had planned. She was sitting at the table sobbing into her hands with the phone beside her. She looked up as I came in. Her eyes were puffy from crying, and the makeup she'd used to hide her bruises was streaked down her face.

"What happened?"

"He's coming."

"Now?"

She shook her head. "Tonight. After the club. He said he wanted..." She bit her lip and the tears started flowing again. "He wanted a special party."

"What does that mean?" I asked, but I knew what it meant. She just closed her eyes and her cheeks shone wet, streaked with makeup. And here I was again, with my arrogance, starting wars and leaving the innocent, broken and weeping, to pick up the pieces of their lives. I had marched into her house, taken on her boyfriend because I didn't like him, taken on Arana because it would be good to bring down the whole damn set-up in one flaming, bleeding mass; play judge, jury, and above all, executioner. But when it no longer suited my plans, I walked away, leaving Cissy defenseless and broken. Just like I was ready to walk away from Marni. Just like I walked away from my home when I was nineteen, to join the British SAS, to go and make war.

Time to stop. Time to do it differently.

"There will be no party tonight, Cissy."

The voice in my head kept telling me this was not my problem, not my fight; to collect my stuff and not make a bad job worse. But I told that voice to shut the fuck up, because as long as I had a shred of humanity left in me, I would not walk away from somebody like Cissy, who needed help. Nobody gets out of here alive. So better to die being a human being, than survive a little longer being a human monster.

"Give me his number."

"What are you going to do?"

"Just give me his number, Cissy."

She told me and I dialed. It rang twice, then Red's voice said, "Who is this?"

"Lacklan. Be at your club tonight at seven forty-five. Be on time. I have a demonstration for you. You're going to like it."

I hung up before he had time to answer. She was watching me. She asked again, "What are you going to do?"

See it through. That was what I was going to do. It had been a mistake to take it on in the first place, but now that I had taken it on, I had to see it through. I had a day, two at the most. It was enough.

I climbed the stairs to my room. She followed me and stood in the doorway as I pulled out my rucksack and started packing it. She saw the Smith & Wesson and the boxes of ammo.

"You're going to kill him, aren't you?"

For the second time that day, I asked her, "Are you sure you want to know, Cissy?"

This time she nodded. "Yes."

"I'm going to kill him."

I stopped what I was doing and we stared at each other for a long moment. Her face was flushed and her eyes were bright. "Good..."

. . .

I DIDN'T LEAVE till late afternoon. I took my things over to Marni's house, put them in the guest room and had a light meal. I didn't know what was going to happen that night, but I was damned sure whatever it was, was going to be the end of it. By tomorrow, one way or another, I planned to be totally focused on Marni and Omega.

I arrived at the Hawk's Nest at seven thirty. At that time it was pretty much empty. I sat at the bar and ordered a whiskey. Red was on time. He stepped through the door with two of his rednecks, saw me and walked over with a look on his face that said he wanted to bullwhip me.

"What's the big idea, Lacklan? You giving me orders now?"

I thought about how to answer him, and while I thought about it I pulled a Pueblo from my pack and lit it. When I'd inhaled deep, I said, "Keep your panties straight, Red. I killed five of Arana's men last night, down at his club in Abasse. Tonight I'm going to kill four more. I figure that gets me a place on the team, what do you say?"

His eyes narrowed. "I say you're full of shit. I got work to do, Lacklan. This what you brought me here for?"

I shook my head. "I told you. I have a demonstration."

"What fuckin' demonstration?"

Right on cue we heard a truck pulling in outside. Only it wasn't just one truck, it was two. Arana was playing it safe. That was fine by me. I climbed off the stool and said, "Come and meet the boys."

Now he looked worried. "What fuckin' boys? What the hell is this, Lacklan?"

I pushed out of the door into the floodlit, dirt forecourt of the club. Red's Ford pick-up was over on the right. On the left, two guys were swinging down from a cream Toyota, and directly in front of us there were four more climbing out of a green Jeep. They were all big and they were all carrying assault rifles. The one who was obviously in charge had a Sancho Panza moustache and a big gut. The other three looked like athletes. Behind me, I heard Red swear, "Holy *shit!*"

Arana's men recognized me from the night before. They thought I was Arana's boy, so they paused and hesitated, probably waiting for instruction. A couple of seconds is all you need.

I had four in front and two on my left. A quick calculation told me the four in front would be getting in each other's way. It was the two on my left flank I needed to worry about.

I threw the knife underhand. It thudded home in the nearest guy's chest and everybody stared at him, while he stared at the hilt sticking out of his sternum. While they all stared I stepped over and took hold of the barrel of the other guy's assault rifle. He stared at me and his expression was almost comical, like he was outraged. I smashed his nose with my left elbow while I slid my right hand down to the trigger. As he staggered back I steadied the barrel and double tapped Sancho Panza, spraying blood and gore out of the back of his chest. So far three seconds had passed.

I put the rifle to my shoulder and took two strides toward them. They were just beginning to react. There were three of them. The nearest was blond with a military crew cut, behind him was a skinny guy with a scar on his face, and next to him was a big slob with long blond hair. He looked real scared. Behind me I was aware of the guy whose nose I'd smashed. He would be reaching for his pal's gun any second.

I took out the crew cut with a double tap that blew the top of his head off. But this was a demonstration. I didn't want to just shoot everybody. So I kicked Scarface in the nuts, smashed Goldilocks in the face with the rifle butt and turned and shot the other guy between the eyes, just as he was reaching for his fallen companion's rifle.

We were far from done yet.

I threw my weapon on the ground. Scarface and Goldilocks were recovering fast. Terror will do that to you. Adrenaline is a powerful medicine. Scarface had a knife in his hand and he lunged at me, snarling. As he did so, I saw Goldilocks reaching for the rifle he'd dropped when I hit him.

It's not like the movies. Fights to the death are very quick, and it is hard to see exactly what happens. Scarface thrust forward with his blade. I deflected his arm inward with my left hand. With my right I took hold of his wrist and folded his arm back against the joint. It happened in a quarter of a second. He lost his footing and dropped the knife. As he fell, I let go of his wrist, put my arm around his throat and twisted. His neck snapped and I was already walking toward Goldilocks before Scarface hit the ground.

He was panicking. I knew he would. That was why I left him till last. He tried to get the rifle trained on me, but before he could, I had levered it out of his hands, smashed him in the head with the butt and emptied two rounds into his chest as he hit the dirt. The whole thing had taken less than twenty seconds.

I dropped the rifle on his chest and walked back toward Red and his two hillbilly goons. He was trying hard not to gape. He was also trying to comprehend what he had just seen.

"Six automatic rifles, two trucks and Arana eleven men down. Does that buy me a place at the table, Red?"

I didn't let him answer. It wasn't really a question. I went and pulled my knife out of the schmuck's chest, wiped it on his shirt and slipped it back in my boot. Red was laughing. It was a kind of hysterical laugh.

"Boy! Boy, you whipped their asses! Man, you just..." He stared around him like he was trying to remember what happened and where. "I didn't see it!" He turned to his goons. "Did you boys see that? I didn't see it!" His voice was shrill in the cold night air, against the sound of distant traffic.

While he was mouthing off, I pulled out my cell and took photographs of the corpses. When I'd finished, I said, "You got a job for me or not, Red?"

His eyes were bright and calculating. "You bet!" He turned to his two gorillas. "Jeb, get this trash cleaned up. Seth, get a couple of boys. You, me, and Lacklan here are going down to collect the merchandise from Romero." To me he grinned and said, "You just got yourself a place on the team, boy."

ELEVEN

WE DROVE FAST THROUGH THE DARK, DOWN THE I-19 toward Nogales. Two bright headlamps in the mirror told us Seth was just behind us. Red was hyped up. He'd been snorting and his adrenaline was pumping hard. I knew the state he was in. I'd never been there myself and never wanted to go. But I'd seen it often enough. It was a dangerous state of mind. He thought he was invincible, indestructible. He wasn't.

At Rio Rico, I made him stop at a gas station so I could use the toilet. After that, we turned left off the interstate and took the South River Road away from the illumination of the town and into the darkness of the desert. We followed the road, winding down to the tiny village of Beyerville, desolate and silent even at this time of night.

Over to the west, there was a glow of some kind of complex or facility on the Santa Cruz river. I didn't know then what it was, or how important it would become.

South of Beyerville, we moved on to a dirt track that bumped and rattled us southeast, toward the border. Pretty soon, we came to the fence and we stopped. In the glow of the headlamps, I could see where somebody had hacked a large gap into it.

"I guess your uncle has friends in the border patrol, huh?"

He laughed and we rolled through. "*Bienvenido a Mexico, amigo!*"

"Where to now?"

"Don't ask questions, Lacklan. Romero does not like questions."

"Romero's your supplier?"

He looked at me with eyes that were cautiously contemptuous in the dark cab. "That another question, Lacklan?"

I met his eye with no particular expression of my own. "You want to shut my mouth for me, Red? Or shall we be friends instead?"

He looked away as we jolted onto a broad dirt track. He didn't answer, but I knew that in that moment he had decided he would have to kill me. A lot of people have decided that about me over the years.

We followed the rough, rutted road through sparse, ghostly trees for about twenty minutes. Then we saw a glow up ahead.

"That's the Romero Ranch."

"Does he make the stuff there?"

He stared at me a moment, his mouth hanging open like he couldn't believe I'd asked another question. Then he sighed.

"Yeah, Lacklan. What are you, CNN? He has a lab in one of the barns. They bring girls in too. They pick 'em up in the ghettos, in the cities." He mused for a moment as we pulled into the drive. "Most times, they're grateful to get out of the slums." He grinned. "At first, anyhow." Then he laughed.

It was a nice ranch, brightly lit, with attractive gardens out front and broad, sweeping stairs up to an elegant, colonial house with shuttered doors under a wide terrace half covered in ivy. There were spotlights concealed among the foliage and in their beams you could see moths spinning insanely in circles, waiting to get eaten by the bats.

Seth pulled up next to us and we climbed out of the trucks. Seth had two rednecks with him, and I saw one of them was carrying a sports bag. The slam of the car doors echoed in the night. Up the steps I saw a group of men standing at the top of the stairs, by the shuttered French doors. The one in the middle had to be Romero. He was small, not more than five-three, in his late fifties with grizzled gray hair and the face of a peasant. He wore jeans and a huntin' shootin' fishin' shirt, riding boots and a cowboy hat. There were four guys with him. They did not seem to be armed, and everybody was smiling. Nobody expected trouble.

As we started up the stairs, Romero came down to greet us.

"Red, good to see you, *amigo. Hola*, Seth!" His eyes flicked over the other guys, whom he clearly recognized, but did not deem worthy of greeting. Then he gave me a once-over and his eyes were hard. He looked into Red's face, gesturing at me with his left hand. "Who is this?"

"This is Lacklan. He's new, Emilio. You're gonna like him..."

Romero raised a hand and shook his head. He didn't look like a man who was about to like anything. He gave a small, humorless laugh. "Don't tell me what I am going to like, Red. What I *don't* like is surprises. You come to my house and you bring somebody I do not know. I don't like this."

Red was uncomfortable and did a funny little dance, jutting out his knees, like he was trying to adjust his pants. "I brought him to introduce you, Emilio. This is one good man."

Romero spread his hands. His face looked constipated. "No, Red, this you tell me *before* you bring him. What do you know about him? Who is he? Where has he lived? What has he done?"

The situation was getting away from me and I was getting mad. I snapped, "Hey! I'm right here, Romero. You got a question, ask me."

He didn't look at me, but he looked like he wanted to gut Red right there and then. His skin seemed to contract over his face and his eyes shone with anger. The boys who'd stayed by the door now came down the steps. I felt the warm glow of adrenaline in my belly and smiled.

"Let me ask you a question, Emilio. You know Arana?"

Red was doing a weird thing with his head. He was staring over to the right, licking his lips. Then he'd turn and stare at nothing on his left, still licking his lips. I just hoped he wasn't going to soil his jeans.

Emilio Romero finally turned and looked at me. "You talkin' to me, *gringo*?"

"Yeah, I'm talking to you. It's a simple question. Do you know Arana? I'm figuring you do, because you're not so stupid that you'd start trafficking *putas* and blow across the border into Arizona without knowing who your competition is. Arana is your competition, and in the last twenty-four hours I have personally killed eleven of his men. So whether you want to or not, Emilio, you are going to like me. Because I am the man who is going give you the Arizona border. You have any questions, you ask me. *Entiendes, compadre?*"

His expression had slowly changed during the speech, from contempt and hatred, to slow understanding. Slow understanding that Red's days were numbered, and I was the guy he needed to be talking to. A faint smile touched his eyes and he looked back at Red. "This is true?"

Red was pale and pasty. He was still doing his weird knee dance and looking at things that weren't there. He nodded. "Sure is, Emilio. I saw him do it with my own eyes. I would never have brought him if I thought you'd feel disrespected. You know that."

Emilio slapped him on the shoulder. "No harm done, my friend. In future..." he turned his smile on me, "In future let's talk *before* we do things. OK, let us go inside."

We followed him up the stairs and through the big doors into a wide, internal patio with a colonnade of arches at ground level and a gallery running around the first floor. There was a fountain playing in the center, illuminated by spots. On the white walls there were wrought iron lamps, and in the small pools of light they gave, I could see geckos, motionless, waiting and watching.

As we crossed the patio toward a door on the far side,

Emilio spoke to me. "Arana is a powerful man. He is very dangerous. But his strength lies mainly in the fact that he is crazy. I have known him for many years, and unless you know him real well, you cannot predict what he is going to do. He rules by terror, instead of by intelligence."

I glanced at him. "But you rule by terror *and* intelligence. That the idea?"

He nodded and spread his hands as he walked. "That *is* the intelligent way." He stopped dead in his tracks and turned to face me. "*Amigo!*" He said it like he was making a really important point, and placed a finger on my chest. "I want you to be terrified of me. Terror is the basis of all power. But not all the time!" He laughed. "Most of the time I want harmony and friendship. But I want you to know, if you cross this line..." he pointed to an imaginary line on the floor. "I will skin you alive!"

I gave him the dead eye to let him know he was teaching his grandmother to suck eggs. "I'll try to remember that."

Over his shoulder I could see Red looking left out. He and Seth glanced at each other. They knew something was wrong but they weren't sure exactly what it was. Emilio nodded and we continued walking. He led us through a door into a kind of dark *bodega*, where there were several barrels against the far wall, a rough-hewn table, a dozen chairs, and cheeses and salamis hanging from the ceiling. He turned and beamed at me. "We do not only make cocaine, Mister Lacklan. We also make wine. The earth is not perfect for vines here, but we are improving, experimenting. I hope one day we will have a good product."

He flipped a switch and gestured to a bench at the far right of the room. Between two pyramids of cheese wheels, there was a stack of plastic packages. It looked oddly homely and inoffensive. I ignored Red, pulled my knife from my boot and stepped over. As I pierced a pack half way down the stash, he elbowed his way toward to me and muttered in my ear, "Take it easy, boy, he's starting to think you're taking over."

I glanced at him like he wasn't real interesting and tasted the blow. I gave Romero something that might have been a smile and said, "*Gasolina!*"

He laughed. "You like it, huh? You got fifteen kilos there. Is good quality. I'm not gonna fuck around givin' you bad shit. I want you to be happy. I want your customers to be happy. When everybody is happy, it means everybody is getting what they want. Am I right?" The question was rhetorical, but he answered himself anyway. It was the kind of man he was. "Of course I'm right." He seemed to remember Red was there and gave him a courtesy smile. "You happy, Red?"

Red sounded peeved. "Yeah, thanks for askin'."

"You wanna see the girls now?"

Red clapped his hands and rubbed them together. "Yeah! And how about a snort on the house, huh, Emilio?" He laughed noisily and Romero turned to one of his boys. "*Traigan a las putas, y unos gramos de coca para los chicos.*"

He gestured to the chairs. "Sit, you want a drink?"

He took a stone jug and filled it from one of the barrels. Seth and Red sat at the table. Their boys stayed standing behind them. Emilio came over with the jug and a handful of tumblers. He was not pretentious. For a moment I thought he was the kind of man who was what he was. He was the kind of man I could have liked, but I put the thought out of my mind. There was no room for that kind of thought in my life. He poured wine and started chopping up a wheel of cheese.

"This is goat's cheese. We feed the goats on rosemary. It gives the cheese a delicate flavor. Try, try."

I sat at the head of the table, took a glass and a piece of cheese. The wine was rough, but he was right, one day it would be good. The cheese was superb. I watched him as I chewed and wondered how a man like this winds up selling human beings for a living.

Dead on cue, there was the sound of heels on tiles and two of Emilio's boys led in six cute young Mexican girls. They all reminded me of Carmencita. They were between fifteen and twenty-two. They were scared, but you could see the fire of hope and defiance in their eyes. Red laughed for no particular reason and stood to go and examine the goods. Seth followed, looking like a hillbilly at a picnic.

Emilio turned to me. "You speak Spanish?"

"Enough."

"*Lo vas a matar?*"

Was I going to kill Red? I let the smile creep onto the right side of my face. "I'm the man you need to be doing business with, Emilio."

"You are dangerous."

"Not as long as we have the same interests."

He made a face that said, 'I guess so'.

Red and Seth came back to the table laughing. Red said, "Sweet, man. Cute babes. I might keep one for me."

"You got the money?"

Seth signaled to the guy with the sports bag, who brought it over and put it on the table. Red opened it.

"Please count it, Emilio. There is one hundred and fifty grand for the coke, and fifteen grand for the girls."

Ten grand a kilo for the coke, two and a half grand each for the girls. Emilio had one of his boys count it. We stayed talking for twenty minutes. Red and Seth had a snort. I ate cheese and Emilio watched me and calculated just how dangerous he thought I was.

By the time we took the coke and the girls out to the trucks, it was almost two AM. We all said goodbye, like we were leaving from an enjoyable dinner party. I half expected Emilio to wave and say, "Do come again!" Instead he said, "I have another fifteen kilos for you in a week."

That was a lot of coke and a lot of girls, and it told me neither was staying in Tucson. Red was planning on moving the stuff nationwide. Which surprised me, because he wasn't smart enough to do that.

The girls rode with Seth in the Jeep, and we went ahead in the pick-up with the coke loaded in the back under a tarpaulin. Red was almost hysterical, pounding the wheel and whooping like a Hollywood cowboy. Like I said, he felt invincible.

"You know what that stuff is worth on the market, boy? You know what that is worth?"

"I know what it's worth."

"You are one miserable son of a bitch, Lacklan, you know that?"

"I know that too."

He laughed and pounded the wheel again. "Man! I am gonna have me a *party* tonight. I am gonna *ride Cissy's ass!*" He laughed some more. "You better get yourself a girl or get out of the house, boy. You ain't gonna sleep tonight, I'm tellin' you that!"

This was his party and nobody was going to rain on it. Not for now, anyway. I smiled. I was thinking of the photographs I had sent Arana from the toilet at Rio Rico, of his dead boys on Red's forecourt, and the message I'd sent with them.

TWELVE

It was four in the morning as we approached the Hawk's Nest along Camino del Oeste. To our right, we could see the orange glow of Tucson. Everywhere else there was the blackness of the empty desert. Except that ahead there was a strange, flickering luminescence. I sat back in my seat and watched his face as it slowly dawned on him that flickering light he was seeing up ahead was dancing flames, and the flashing red and blue of fire trucks and police cars.

"*What the motherfucking...?*"

We pulled in to the forecourt and he leapt from the cab. Everything was flooded in a wavering, orange glow from the tall flames that were reaching up into the blackness, and trailing sparks and embers like a dragon's tail out into the night. But from what I could see, the blaze was coming mainly from a group of outhouses and sheds at the back, not so much the concrete structure of the club itself. A concrete building is hard to ignite, and I figured Arana's boys had been in a hurry. There were two trucks there and a half-dozen guys dousing everything in water.

Red stood staring, with his arms flung wide in a gesture of helplessness. I watched a couple of cops and the sheriff of San Juan, out of his jurisdiction, walking toward him. I waited to see what would happen. Red turned to them as they approached, shouting above the roar of the flames. "What the fuck? *What the fuck, man?*"

I heard one of the cops say, "I thought you'd want me to call your uncle Caleb…"

Sheriff Caleb was saying, "You any idea who would want to do this, Red…?"

I climbed out of the pick-up and slammed the door loud enough to be heard. The cop and the sheriff both looked over. I saw the sheriff's face harden. I paused to light a cigarette and strolled over, keeping my eyes on Sheriff Caleb's. I repeated his words as I drew closer, "Any idea who might have done this…?"

He spoke half to himself. "What the hell…?"

"You're a little out of your jurisdiction, aren't you, Sheriff?" Before he could answer, I turned to Red. "Looks like you got a leaky appliance somewhere, Red." I eyed the lawman sidelong. "Leaky appliances can be real dangerous. People can get hurt, and even killed. What do you say, Sheriff? Would you say it's important to shut off any leaky appliances?"

"Who is this clown, Red?"

Red wasn't listening. He had his hands to his head and the light from the leaping flames made him look like a distressed minor devil in a remote corner of hell.

"What makes you call me a clown, Sheriff? Clowns make

people laugh. I haven't made anybody laugh." I raised my voice. "Red!" He turned to face me. He was out of control. "This was an accident. A leak. And that's what the fire department is going to find. You don't need the cops here, do you?"

The meaning of my words began to sink in. He nodded. "Yeah. No. This weren't arson, Sergeant. For sure. This was not arson."

The sergeant gave me a once-over, then turned to Sheriff Caleb. "Stay in touch, Caleb. Let me know if anything develops, will you?"

"Sure."

He walked away and had a word with the chief fireman. He'd wait for the report. By the time he got the report, I'd be long gone. The sheriff was talking to Red again. "Who the fuck is this, Red?"

He jabbed his thumb at me.

"He's my associate, uncle Caleb. What the hell happened here?"

I answered him, but I was looking at his uncle. "What's happened here is that somebody has been talking to Arana."

Red stared at me. "You!" he said, simply. His uncle leered at me and he went on. "You. It must be you. How else did you get six of his men to show up here...?"

I narrowed my eyes at him, "Jesus, Red! You know? Try thinking sometimes. I told him I had a couple of Ks of marijuana to sell him. I gave him this spot as a remote place to meet. I wanted to set up a demonstration for you, pal! Why would I waste six of his guys and then have him firebomb you? Use your fucking brain sometimes!"

He looked mad. "OK! Take it easy!"

Sheriff Caleb was looking very sick. "I'm asking you again, Red. Who the *fuck* is this guy?"

I answered for him. "I'm his guardian angel, Caleb. I've come to fix the leak. You heard from Arana lately, Sheriff?"

"What are you talking about?"

I gave him my nastiest smile. "I plugged a couple of leaks at the *Casa Coca* just last night. I thought Arana might have called you in." I shrugged and laid on the deep south drawl. "You bein' the local sheriff an'all."

He swallowed hard. "You playin' with fire boy."

I looked past him and the blaze. "Somebody sure is." I turned to Red. "Somebody has told Arana about your operation. You have a leak that needs plugging, fast. You got somewhere you can stay for a couple of days?"

He shrugged. "I could stay at Seth's..."

"Do that. I'm going to take care of this for you. I'll contact you when it's all clear." I took a long moment to look into the sheriff's eyes. "If Arana finds out you are Red's uncle, you could be seriously at risk, Sheriff. I would advise you to keep a low profile for a day or two."

He tried a little bluster, but it wasn't very convincing. "I ain't scared of no..."

"You should be. Take my advice." To Red I said, "I'm going to need Seth and two of your toughest boys. I'm going to make Arana wish he'd never been born." I leered at Sheriff Caleb. "Don't you go ratting me out now, Caleb, will you? I am pretty sure Arana is not your friend right now."

He went very pale and shook his head. "No, why would I...?"

My voice was almost a whisper, "Where does he live, Sheriff?"

"He kind of moves about, Mexico, LA..."

"When he's here, where does he live?"

"He's got a penthouse at the casino, but he prefers the *Casa Coca.* The top floor is an apartment. It's real luxurious. He says he gets privacy there, and it's right on the border..."

His voice trailed away.

"You seem to know him pretty well."

He shook his head quickly. "No, not really..."

"Is that where he is now?"

"I guess it is."

"Go home, sheriff. Now. I'll be in touch."

He turned and hurried away toward his truck. He crossed the fire chief coming the other way. The fire was dying down and the main building of the club didn't look too badly damaged.

"I hope you had your stores insured, Red. You're going to have to restock the place. The good news is you have a place to restock. Pure luck, a passing motorist saw the fire and called it in. If we'd arrived twenty minutes later, the whole place would've been a write off. I figure this afternoon you should be able to get in there."

Red was sinking fast after his high.

I said, "You got somewhere for the girls?"

He looked confused. "Yeah, yeah. I got it."

"I'll call you later." I left him with the fire chief and went over to the Jeep. It was another hour and a half till dawn and the sky was black. I wrenched open the passenger door. Seth and the guys gawped at me. Seth said, "What's goin' on?"

"You're with me. We're going to pay a visit to Arana. You two, get in the back of the pick-up."

"Now?"

"Yeah, now."

They didn't question it. They sighed and groaned and climbed down. Seth was running his fingers though his short hair. "Man! I am so done. I need to sleep."

"You'll sleep when you're dead," I said. "Now get in the fucking truck."

The two guys climbed in the back and Seth got in next to me in the cab. I fired up the engine and hammered out of the forecourt in a cloud of dust. In the rearview, I could see Red staring after me. It had dawned on him too late that the coke was still in the truck.

I drove across town toward Marni's place. I was making it up as I went along, but I was getting a good feeling. I thought maybe I'd have the whole damn thing wrapped up within twenty-four hours.

The first gray tints of dawn were touching the east as I pulled up on Brooks Drive. I snarled, "Stay here. Don't move," climbed out, and sprinted over to the house. I let myself in. It was still and dark, and very quiet. I climbed the stairs to my room, pulled out the Smith & Wesson 500 cannon, the pack of C4 and the detonators, and stuffed them all in my rucksack. I smiled. Things were going to get intense. I was doing what I was good at, and that always made me smile.

Two minutes later, I was climbing back in the cab.

"OK, Seth," I said. "Let's go reap the harvest."

He looked at me like all he wanted to do was sleep. I laughed, turned west onto Stella and floored the pedal toward Valencia Road, and Three Points.

THIRTEEN

The sun was bleeding molten copper over the high sierras in the east when we finally rolled into Abasse. Seth had fallen asleep, and I was willing to guess the two guys in the back were out for the count too. I didn't know how many guys Arana had with him. I didn't know if he had anybody with him. I didn't know a damn thing. I was flying by the seat of my pants and trying to be creative.

I glanced at Seth. He had a Springfield XD in his waistband. I figured the two in the back had something similar. I saw the sign for the *Casa Coca*, slowed and pulled in. The bouncing on the dirt track woke him and he looked around, steadying himself against the door and the dash.

"We arrived, Seth. This is your appointment with destiny."

He frowned at me like he thought I was crazy. "Man, can I get some coffee somewhere?"

"Nope." I pulled up and killed the engine. "Let's go. There are people to kill."

I climbed down and heard him clamber out the other side. I walked toward the tailgate, hammering on the truck. "C'mon, guys! There's work to be done. Wake up!"

I figured whoever was in the house would be hearing the noise, and that suited me fine. As the two sleepy schmucks yawned and stretched and slid down from the back, I held out my hand. "Let me see your weapons," I said, like I was going to check them out.

They pulled out two automatics, a Desert Eagle and a Glock 43. Two nice guns. I examined them and called to Seth, "Seth! C'mere! Let me see your Springfield."

He started shambling toward me and I was aware of one of the shutters moving on the top story of the building. It only moved a couple of inches, but it was enough for me to see it.

The sun was over the horizon now and a warming breeze was stirring. Seth handed me his pistol. It was a 9mm. I put it and the Colt in my waistband, cocked the Glock 43, flipped off the safety and aimed at Seth's head. "All of you, turn around, put your hands on your heads, take five steps toward the house and get on your knees. Do as I say and you get to go home tonight."

Seth said, "Oh, God..." and did as he was told. All three of them lined up with their backs to me and their elbows sticking out like Mickey Mouse ears and shambled nervously up toward the house. They were too damned lazy to think, they were used to doing what they were told, and they weren't smart enough to question what I was telling them. When they were twenty-five feet from the porch, I said, "Stop. Now get on your knees." They did it.

I could hear Seth whimpering, "Oh God...".

Then I bellowed at the top of my lungs.

"*Arana! You got a fucking leak! What kind of shit operation are you running? They knew your guys were coming! They wiped them out and you almost got me killed, you motherfucker! Now I am going to give you one more chance, you Mickey Mouse piece of fucking shit! Come out here and be a witness to this!*"

I waited a couple of minutes. I knew he would come and he did. Eventually the door creaked and he stepped out onto the porch in his dressing gown and slippers, carrying a shot gun.

"You got some fuckin' nerve showin' up around here..."

I snarled at him, "Yeah, we'll talk about that. Do you know who these guys are?"

He nodded. "This one is Seth, that is Bobby and he is Sam. They run with Red, so what?"

They nodded back at him, like the fact that he knew them would make a difference. It was sad. I nodded too. We were all nodding.

"The same Red who just tonight collected fifteen kilos of blow from Emilio Romero, south of the border. Fifteen kilos of blow and six *muchachas* for his whore house. The same Red who will take delivery of another, similar load next week, right under your fucking nose. The same Red whose uncle is Sheriff Caleb of San Juan County—your fucking county! I told you he was a rat and what the *fuck* have you done about it?"

He was almost apologetic. "I send some boys to his house. He was not there..."

"Do you know what *fucking incompetent* means, Arana?"

Now he looked mad. "Come on! I lost eleven men in two nights! Good men don't grow on fuckin' trees!"

I shot Seth in the back of the head. It was a hollow tip .45 so his face exploded over the dust. It seemed to shock Arana. I shot the other two in rapid succession. I pointed at the three corpses. "That evens things up a little. Now come here." I walked back to the pick-up and pulled off the tarp to expose the fifteen kilos of coke. Arana walked up slow, with his slippers dragging in the dust. He stood staring at it. I pulled one of the packs out and handed it to him. "Try it."

He did and made a face of approval. "Is good. Is good stuff."

"I know. Now, are you willing to trust me?"

"How much is here?"

"I told you. Fifteen K." I looked around like I was distressed. "Where are your fucking men, Arana? What kind of piss operation are you running? I could have killed you fifteen times over!"

He shrugged. "Chill, *gringo*! They are asleep. We had a party last night. We weren't expecting no focking crazy killers this morning. We torched Red's place, then we partied." He grinned. "That's how we roll in Mexico. Fifteen kilos, huh?" He did the math. "That is a street value of two and a quarter million."

"Yeah, but only if you're alive. Romero has a good organization, and when he and Red wake up to what's going down they'll be all over you like cheap whores on a sailor. You need to get your shit together, Arana."

"OK, OK... Come on, let's get some coffee. We'll get

the boys to bring this in." I followed him towards the house and was surprised to see he was creasing up, laughing. "You are one crazy motherfocker. One day I maybe have to kill you, but I will regret it. I like you. You out of your fockin' mind." He gestured back at the bodies and at the truck. "You turn up at my house like this at seven in the morning..." His laugh was almost a giggle. "You fockin' crazy!"

I read once that the average IQ of a criminal is between 80 and 90. It made sense. I sighed. "Yeah. It's hilarious."

Inside he started shouting his head off. "*Venga! Pendejos! Levántense! Que no sirven para nada, hijos de puta! A levantarse ya!*"

All of which basically meant, get up.

Within twenty minutes, the place was full of slightly green-looking Mexicans asking, "*Que paso?*" and scratching their heads. Arana dispatched four of them to get rid of Seth and his pals, and for a bit there was a lot of retching going on outside, then cursing and laughing, and finally the sound of a truck pulling out and somebody hosing down the yard.

Meanwhile, a couple of girls had made coffee and were scrambling eggs in the kitchen. Arana and I sat at a table to eat breakfast and he spread his hands. "OK, so tell me, what's going on?"

"I'll tell you what's going on in three simple sentences. Red is moving in on your patch. He is being supplied by Emilio Romero, ten miles southeast of Nogales. His uncle, Sheriff Caleb, is helping him by feeding him information about you." I pulled out my cigarettes and lit up while he poured Tabasco sauce on his scrambled eggs. "I want to work with you, Arana. You have the organization and I have the talent. We can take over the show, but you have to get serious."

He made a face like I was being boring, but nodded anyway. "You right, I know. I know you right. But you gotta question, sometimes, your values in life. If you are successful but you are not happy no more, are you successful *at all?*"

He spread out his hands and stared at me, like he'd asked a really important question. I watched him till he started eating again.

"You need to get rid of the sheriff and replace him with somebody you can trust. You need to get rid of Red and you need to destroy his supplier. *He* is your biggest problem. Red and his uncle are stupid, but Romero is smart, efficient and well organized."

"You met him?"

"I was at his ranch last night collecting your coke and six whores."

"Where are the *putas*?"

"In Tucson, at what's left of Red's club."

He stuffed the last of his eggs in his mouth, swallowed and drained his coffee. He shouted, "*Traigan mas café, oigan!*" and sat back to consider me. Finally he shrugged. "OK, so what you wanna do? I lost a lot of men thanks to you. I can't afford a gang war on two fronts."

"You don't need a lot of men, and you don't need a gang war on any fronts. You need to destroy them, not fight with them. How many boys you got left?"

He gestured at the door. "Pepe, Juan and Julio, who went to bury Seth. And here we got Alejando, Nelson and Chico. That's all I got left."

"What about the suit who was here the other night?"

"He's my attorney. I got him on a retainer."

"Give me your four best guys. I'll take them down to Romero's ranch tonight. We'll kill him and destroy his operation. Whoever your supplier is, he'll be grateful. If I were you, I'd be asking him how the hell he let this fucking bozo get this far in the first place."

He grunted. "Don't create problems with my supplier, *gringo*. He is very powerful and very dangerous."

"Who is he?"

He studied my face. He looked sour. He didn't like all my questions and he didn't like that I was taking control. He shrugged. "Rafael Montilla. He is part of the Sinaloa cartel." He laughed. "You don't wanna make them unhappy, *gringo*. They pretty much run Mexico. And I ain't talkin' about the criminal underworld. I am talking about *Mexico!*"

"That powerful, huh?" I showed him I was skeptical by raising an eyebrow.

"*Amigo*, when I tell you that they own the whole fockin' west of the country from Tijuana and Mexicali to Acapulco, and that their plantations of marijuana and coca..." He paused to lean forward and touch my shoulder, like he was trying to make me pay attention. "Their plantation cover more than twenty-three *thousand miles*—that is bigger than Costa Rica. These are official figures, *amigo*. Check them if you don't believe me."

"Your guy Rafael represents this organization?"

"This organization? You kidding me? Is the biggest focking drugs cartel in the world. Where you fockin been for the last ten years?"

"Wyoming. Are we on or what?"

"Tonight?"

"Why wait?"

He laughed. "Sure, why not?"

One of the girls came out of the kitchen with another pot of coffee. She was trying hard to smile, but she looked wrecked. Outside I heard the truck return with Pepe, Juan and Julio. I sighed. "OK, assemble your men and we'll go over the plan."

FOURTEEN

THE PLAN WAS SIMPLE. EXECUTING IT WITH FOUR mental retards would not be. The SAS operates with units of four men who are smart enough and well-trained enough to cause mayhem and devastation on a scale you'd normally associate with an entire armored division. But each soldier in the SAS is chosen for his intelligence and commitment. The guys I had here were like a gang of lobotomized moral philosophers at a cannabis convention. So the plan had to be simple.

I'd selected Pepe, Nelson, Julio, and Chico. They were the least stupid and the least hungover. Nelson was skinny and psychotic and had a mustache he'd inherited from his father in the 1970s. Chico was small and tattooed and liked to play with knives. Julio was big, black and tattooed, and also liked to play with knives. Pepe was the brains of the outfit. He looked normal and could spell his name without poking out his tongue.

Mid-morning, we took two trucks and crossed into

Mexico at Abasse, two minutes down the road from the *Casa Coca*. Then we drove east, taking the remote back roads, for thirty miles across the desert to Nogales. At Nogales, we took route 15 south to Cibuta and crossed the high mesa by winding mountain roads till we came out, early afternoon, in the Santa Cruz river valley, half a mile south of Romero's ranch.

There we had lunch and reviewed the plan. They sighed a lot, like I was being boring. Mexican *banditos* as a rule all have two plans, whatever the operation: plan A and plan B. Plan A is shoot everything. Plan B is, if plan A doesn't work, run.

This plan was a little more complicated. Romero's ranch sat on five acres of fertile land on the west bank of the Santa Cruz river, at the foot of the hills that rose up into the high mesa. It was fenced and shielded from the road by tall poplars and cypresses. The house itself was large and built around a central patio, but to the west and the south there were four large, wooden structures that looked like barns. I was pretty sure they housed the labs where he made the coke and the crack, and I was willing to bet there was also a place where he kept the less willing girls, the ones who were a flight risk.

What I wanted to do was position Pepe and his pals around the barns, covering the exit from the house. Then I wanted to start a fire in one of the barns. When Romero and his men emerged to put out the blaze, we'd pick them off, close in on the house and finish the job.

Simple.

I explained it to them. They shrugged a lot and said OK. We'd brought automatic rifles, and I had my rucksack with me for a grand finale. We ate some bread and cheese and then laid up in the hills for the guys to get some sleep till dusk.

While they slept, I watched the ranch and made a note of all the people that I saw. There wasn't a lot of activity. I saw a couple of guys make repeat visits to the northernmost barn, and once it looked like they were carrying food. My money was on the girls being imprisoned in there.

By late afternoon, I had made out a total of eight guys, but I figured there could be between two and four inside, which would bring it to ten or twelve total. That meant, worst case, we were outnumbered three to one. If I'd been with a team from the Regiment, I'd like those odds. Right now it felt more like I was outnumbered twelve to one.

As dusk fell, I kicked the guys awake, gave them coffee, and led them out of the foothills and up to the trees by the fence south of the ranch. The nearest barn stood about fifty feet away. The only person I'd seen go in there all day was a farm hand who'd collected four bales of hay in a pick-up and taken them across the road to some horses by the river. That had confirmed my choice for where to start my fire. It also narrowed down the location of the lab. It had to be in one of the other three barns on the left. And I'd eliminated one of those as housing the girls.

By now, dusk was falling and darkness was seeping into the air. I could see the warm amber of lamps coming on in the windows. I spoke quietly and slowly.

"Pepe, you're going to take Chico and you're going to go to the farthest barn, where you can see the front of the house. You're going to stay low, OK? Meanwhile, Nelson, you and Julio are going to go to the second building, where you can cover the front of this nearest barn, where they keep the hay. *Comprende?*"

They nodded. "Is easy, boss. We ain't stupid."

"Shut up, Pepe. Now, I am going to start a fire in the hay barn. Pepe, when you and Chico count eight guys out of the house, then you start shooting. *Not* before. You got that?"

He rolled his eyes. "Count eight. Then shoot."

"Nelson, Julio, *only* when Pepe and Chico start shooting, then you start. That way, you trap them in a killing field. When they are dead, you meet me at the front of the house. Stay low, there may be more guys inside." They all nodded again. "OK, Pepe, you and Chico, go!"

They slipped through the trees and over the fence and made their way around the back of the barns. I gave them thirty seconds, then Nelson, Julio and I followed. I dispatched them to the second structure and told them to stay low and silent. Meanwhile, I crawled to the big doors and eased them open just enough for me to squeeze in. I stayed there by the entrance and counted to thirty, allowing my eyes to adjust to the dark. Then I looked around.

There were no animals there. It was basically two large stacks of hay bales, from floor to ceiling. It was perfect. I went to the back of the barn, flipped my Zippo and set light to the bottom-most bale. Then I ran.

It was thirty yards from the barn to the back of the house. I covered the distance at a crouching sprint and took up my position, lying on my belly directly opposite Nelson and Julio, and facing the big doors. Once Romero's men were at the barn they'd have fire in front of them, me, Nelson and Julio on either side, and Pepe and Chico behind them. It would be a death trap.

Pretty soon there was thick smoke billowing out of the wooden structure, stretching out like a long, black sausage toward the river. Then there were a couple of '*whoof!*' sounds, big flames erupted from the sides and started licking up the walls toward the roof, and a drifting stream of flaming cinders trailed across the ranch, threatening to ignite anything in its path.

Now.

There were shouts from the house. Like the barn, they ignited, and next thing it was panic, running feet and voices screaming for water. One thing they would not do was call the fire department or the cops, not with a coke and meth factory on the premises. This would be a hoses and buckets job. With a delivery due in a few days, Romero had to be freaking. It took them all of five minutes to get organized. Pepe and Chico were as good as their word and held their fire.

Then they arrived, ten of them, forming a human chain, hurling ineffectual buckets of water at what had become an inferno, screaming ineffectual instructions about how to stop it spreading. The roar of the flames almost drowned out the staccato spit of the assault rifles as they opened up, and the first two guys stumbled and fell.

Then Nelson, Julio and I opened up too. It was a steady rain of fire, and they didn't stand a chance. They were unarmed, unprepared and, above all, unsuspecting. In the infernal, wavering orange glow of the towering flames, their shadows, cast long and black, danced and jerked as they were struck on three sides by hot, flying lead. Whichever way they ran there was no shelter, no refuge, no way out. No hope.

We cut them down without mercy. It was all over within fifteen or twenty seconds.

I didn't wait. I was on my feet and running, changing the magazine. I skirted the house on the western side and headed for the front door, where Red and I had pulled up just a day earlier.

I took cover behind a poplar and saw Pepe and Chico approaching at a crouch on the far side. They were grinning and gave me the thumbs-up. Behind them, I saw Nelson and Julio. I signaled Nelson and Pepe to join me and they ran over.

I spoke as they hunkered down. "I didn't see Emilio out there. So I am figuring he's inside. He's smart, so he's taken up a position up in the gallery, covering the entrance."

Pepe nodded. "OK, boss, makes sense."

"I want you and the boys to take up a position by the door. Draw their fire. Keep them pinned down." I pointed at the terrace above the entrance. "I'm going up there and I'm going to hit them in the flank. My guess is there are four of them at most."

They looked doubtfully at the terrace. I said, "Go!" They called Chico and Julio and the four of them ran toward the tall French doors. I sprinted across the garden, jumped, grabbed the ivy and hauled myself up onto the terrace. I lay a moment listening, and watching the sparks trail across space like an incandescent, drifting galaxy. The only sound was the roar of the flames.

Then there was the stutter of automatic fire. I got up and made for the plate glass doors. There was only blackness on the other side. I pulled my Sig, screwed on the silencer, and put a round through the glass. Then I reached in and released the lock.

I was in a large, overly ornate drawing room in a vulgar, pseudo-rococo style. It was still and dark, and somehow the stammering sound of gunfire outside the door made it seem quiet on the inside. There were two doors, one on either side of the fireplace. I made a 3D mental map of the building and figured that, if they were covering the entrance, as they obviously were, the door on the right would give me a direct line of fire on their flank. And from what I remembered of the gallery, they would be no more than forty feet away. I dropped my rucksack on a fake Louis XV sofa and pulled out the Smith & Wesson 500 cannon. It is an obscene revolver that uses a seven hundred grain bullet that will bust through body armor and shatter concrete.

In moments of high stress and danger, people react instantly to sudden violent movements. But what is not widely understood is that calm, deliberate movements in moments of high stress and danger can be very confusing. Your brain just doesn't process them. It's a fact I have used many times to my advantage.

FIFTEEN

I OPENED THE DOOR AND SAW THEM. THEY HAD pulled out furniture, piled it along the rails of the gallery, and were shooting over the top of it at Pepe and his pals down below. I hadn't wrenched the door open and stormed out. I just opened it calmly and took aim while they stared at me in astonishment. There were five of them, including Emilio.

The first round tore through the nearest guy's chest, blasting blood and gore all over his friends and tearing out the belly of the guy behind him, before smashing into the barricade of furniture and sending splinters showering into the air. Emilio and his two *compadres* cowered away from the noise and violence of the Smith & Wesson. I lined up the second shot, sparing Emilio till last, and took off the other two guys' heads like a couple of exploding watermelons.

Emilio dropped onto his knees. I took three steps toward him. "Who's left, Emilio?"

"Nobody. Is just me. Why? You? The merchandise was good. I making more. What happen?"

"It's a long story." I raised my voice. "*Cease fire! Cease fire!*" The shooting stopped. I shouted again. "*We're clear! Upstairs!*"

There was the tramp of feet across the indoor patio followed by the stomp of boots on the stairs. I pulled out my pack of Pueblos, lit one and handed it to Emilio as the boys arrived. He took it with trembling hands and sucked on it. "Who are you?"

I nodded, like I thought it was a good question. "I'm a double-edged blade, Emilio. One side is the judge, and the other is the executioner. You have any girls here right now?"

He nodded. "Three. In the nearest barn."

I turned to Pepe. "Take Chico. Let them out and bring them to the front of the house. Stay with them." He nodded and went to leave. I stopped him. "Pepe?" He turned. "If you hurt them I will cut your arms off. I'm serious. Treat them with respect."

He gaped a bit, then nodded. "OK."

That left me, Nelson, Julio, and Emilio. I turned back to Emilio. "You got money on the premises?" He sighed. I said, "Think carefully about your answer, Emilio. I like you. You want to keep me well disposed toward you."

"Yeah, in the safe. The money you brought yesterday, plus a hundred grand in US dollars." He shrugged. "Three hundred and sixty-five grand. Maybe a bit more."

I jerked my head. "Let's go."

He led the way along the gallery to the corner room. It was a comfortable, Castilian style study with a big, oak desk, a huge sofa and tall bookcases. I saw several books on wine.

Through the window, I could see the crazy glow of the fire raging out back. The safe was unconcealed, standing in the corner. He got down and opened it, pulled the money out and stacked it on the desk. I looked at Julio and pointed back along the gallery.

"I left my rucksack in the room at the end. It's on the sofa. Go get it for me."

He walked out of the office. I gave him fifteen seconds to get there. I had three rounds left in the Smith & Wesson. I blew Emilio's heart out of the back of his ribcage all over the window. It made the glow of the fire turn red and black across the glass. Nelson was gaping in surprise when I blew his head off his shoulders.

Buddhists say that your dying thought conditions how you are reborn. I guess Nelson will come back as an astonished baby. I shouted loud and urgent out of the door.

"Julio! Get back here! Now!"

I heard him lumbering down the gallery and as he came through the door I cut him in half with the last round. The two bits of him lay in an ocean of blood, twitching. It was odd that the twitches in his hands were in sync with the twitches in his legs, even though they were no longer connected. He also had a 'what the hell' look on his face. I'd done my bit towards creating a generation of wonder.

He'd brought my rucksack with him, so I removed Romero's head with my knife, wrapped it in his shirt and stuffed it, along with the money, in the sack. I didn't enjoy doing it, but sometimes you have to do unpleasant things in life. That's just the way it is. I made my way down the stairs. On the way, I rummaged through the pockets of the various corpses, collecting car keys. That wasn't nice either.

I found Pepe and Chico standing with the three girls out front, in the wavering orange light of the fire. Chico was trying to have a conversation with them, like he was chatting them up on a street corner, raising his voice over the roar and crackle. The girls were lined up in a row, staring at him like he was crazy.

I'd put the Smith & Wesson in the rucksack. I didn't figure I would need it again that night. I had the Sig p226 under my arm. That would be a different story. I spoke as I approached them.

"Any of you girls know how to drive?" They gawped at me, either because they were in shock, or because they didn't speak English. I tried again. "*Quien de ustedes sabe manejar?*"

One of them, she looked like the oldest, raised her hand. "*Yo se manejar. Tengo permiso.*"

She had a license. I looked at the guys and pointed at the barns. "Those two barns, where you didn't find the girls?" They looked and nodded. "One of them is a lab. Go have a look. See if there's a stash there."

They nodded again and set off at a run. When they'd gone inside, I pulled out thirty grand from the rucksack and gave the girls ten grand each, plus the keys to an Audi. I pointed at the cars parked out front. "Get the hell out of here. *Váyanse! Váyanse rápido!*"

They just stood and gaped. Today was a day for gaping. "Go! *Go!*"

Finally they turned and ran toward the car, glancing over their shoulders at me like I might shoot them in the back before they got away. I ignored them and headed after Pepe and Chico at a jog. My job tonight was almost done.

As I pushed through the door into the middle barn, I

heard the Audi sliding away onto the road. I tried not to think of all the things that could go wrong for three young girls in a stolen Audi with thirty thousand US dollars between them. I told myself, if they were smart, they had a fighting chance. Which was more than Pepe and Chico had.

I stood looking around. They'd found the light switch and the big, fluorescent overhead lamps were casting a dull, dead light over the cavernous wooden hangar. It was a big operation. There were benches, easily forty feet long, where the blocks of coke were already being stacked. I counted twenty kilos just at a glance. Pepe and Chico were watching me, waiting for instructions. They were surprised, like me. I was asking myself, if the Sinaloa cartel was so powerful, and this ranch was firmly inside their territory, how the hell had Romero got away with setting up such a big operation?

Looking at the equipment and the raw materials he had amassed, he was either preparing to give the cartel a run for its money, or they knew what he was doing and were on board with it. To give a cartel pulling in four billion bucks a year a run for its money is, at best, a stupid thing to do. And Emilio had not been a stupid man. So there was more going on here than I was aware of. Suddenly, I had alarm bells going off in my head.

Pepe shrugged and spread his hands. "What the hell, boss?"

I pulled the Sig and said, "I'm not your boss, Pepe, I'm your executioner."

His reflexes were better than I expected. He lunged to one side, hit the floor in a roll, and ran screaming behind one of the benches as the Sig spat and two rounds hit the floor. I swore under my breath. Chico reached for his gun and joined the ranks of gaping souls waiting to be reborn as surprised babies.

I went after Pepe, but he was scrambling around like a headless chicken on speed. I let off two more rounds and missed again. Then he was bolting through the door.

Now I had a problem. I needed to destroy the lab, but I needed to get Pepe before he made it back to Arana. I needed Arana on side, and talking. That meant I had to act fast.

I ran to the door. What I did next depended on what direction he took. If he went left to grab one of the cars at the front of the house, I'd follow and kill. If he went right, over the fence and back toward where we'd left the trucks, I'd let him get away, finish the work in hand, and then hunt him down in the sierra. That would be a problem.

He did what he'd probably been doing all his life. He made the wrong choice. He ran for the cars. In the light of the collapsed hay barn, now burning low and starting to smolder, he was a dancing, jerking black silhouette. I ran five strides and dropped on one knee. I took my time, a full two seconds to aim, then double-tapped.

I saw him stumble, then heard him swear, "*Ay, mierda!*" He took another step and then carefully lay down. I jogged over and confirmed the kill with a round to the back of the head. In his next life, he would be a disgruntled baby. Shit happens.

I went back into the lab, pulling the C4 from my rucksack as I went. I broke the cake in two and placed one half dead center on the stash of coke on the bench. I set the detonator to ignite in half an hour and ran. I was figuring that on a remote ranch like this, there had to be a store of fuel for the trucks. As you'd expect, it hadn't been with the hay. It hadn't been with the girls or in the lab either. That only left the barn next door.

I wrenched open the big, wooden doors and sure enough, they had half a dozen drums stashed against one wall, beside a truck and a tractor. Fighting to stay focused, I shaped the other half of the C4 and placed it on the lower middle drum. I set the detonator for twenty-seven minutes.

For good measure, on my way out, I passed by the kitchen in the house and opened all the gas taps. Houses in Mexico, especially in the country, tend to use large canisters of propane to heat their water and to cook. Propane is highly explosive and it ignites very easily. I now had a large house filling up with combustible gas, a burning barn, half a dozen drums of gasoline and two shaped charges of C4, all ready to go off at the same time—in about fifteen minutes.

It was time to go.

I ran, sprinting back across the open land, past the smoldering wreck of the hay barn, over the fence and away. Now my mind was focused on Arana. I kept thinking about what he'd said about his supplier, Rafael Montilla, connected to the Sinaloa cartel. Something was nagging at my mind, something that didn't make sense. My mind was spinning, racing, making connections.

Connections that should not be possible.

SIXTEEN

AFTER TEN MINUTES OF SCRAMBLING THROUGH the undergrowth and clambering over rocks, I crested a hill and paused to catch my breath. Three distinct reports in rapid succession tore the night in half. The first was the flat, jarring slam of C4. I turned to look and saw the lab building disintegrating by the dim light of the hay barn. A second later, there was the richer, deeper roar of gasoline igniting, and the next barn went up in a mushroom fireball that illuminated the whole ranch and tore through what was left of the barns, sending out liquid tongues of fire toward the sky and the house.

Then came the third explosion: the hard, flat bang of gas shattering the roof and the windows of the house, sending blue plumes of translucent flame curling out into the darkness. I didn't pause to see the aftermath. The job was done. Below me, I could see the glint of reflected fire on the chassis of the Jeep. I bounded down, staggering, slipping and sliding, crashing through the small trees and bushes, toward the esplanade in the gully where we had left the trucks.

I drove hard, chasing the funnels of the headlamps around the tight twists and hairpin bends of the road. Climbing higher into the sierra. I could have taken the 195 through Nogales, and that would have been quicker, but I didn't fancy driving through populated places with US plates and a Mexican head in my rucksack, in the vicinity of a large explosion. It didn't seem smart.

It was close to eleven PM as I pulled in to the parking lot at the *Casa Coca*. I climbed out of the cab and stood for a moment to light a cigarette and look up at the translucent emptiness of the night sky, peppered by a trillion specs of frozen light. I told myself there was no heaven up there that we could aspire to, no hell beneath us that could be condemned to. We were not suspended between Heaven and Hell. We were in Hell, plain and simple. We were in Hell, trying to get out.

I crossed to the door and pushed through. Arana was sitting at his usual table with Juan and Alejandro, his two last remaining boys, drinking beer and playing cards. The bar was quiet, aside from the wailing of a Mexican band and a couple of girls sitting and talking at the bar.

They looked up as I walked in and threw the rucksack on the table. It landed with a hard thud. They all stared at it.

"Open it."

His fingers fumbled with the buckles, but he finally got it open and Romero's head rolled out, wrapped in the sticky, bloody shirt, followed by a drift of hundred dollar bills. He peeled back the shirt and looked at the features.

I asked, "Do you know him?"

He glanced at me, then looked back at the waxy face. He shrugged. "Emilio... Yeah, I think so... His face is familiar."

"The money was in the safe. It's what Red paid him for the coke. Now you got the coke, the money, and Red's supplier. It's a good day for you. You happy yet?"

I walked to the bar and told Anita, one of the girls, to get me a cold beer. I sat on a stool and turned to face him. He was watching me. He had a curious expression on his face. "Where are Pepe, Chico, Julio, Nelson..."

"They were incompetent. They got killed. I destroyed the lab, burned down the ranch."

He narrowed his eyes and shook his head. "There is something wrong with you, *gringo*. You're like a one-man focking holocaust, destroyin' everything. Everywhere you go, people die." He shook his head again, more emphatically. "You know what? Take the money. Fock off. I don't want you round here. You're fockin' dangerous."

I picked up the beer Anita had put on the bar and smiled at him.

"Too hot for you, Arana?"

"Fock you."

"When we're done, I'll go."

Juan and Alejandro were looking nervous. Arana said, "When we are done? I just told you, we're done."

I swigged and sighed. It felt good. I was tired. "I need to get rid of Red, remember? Leave you in control down here. Then you pay me off..." I pointed at the bag. "Whatever's in there. And I blow town, leaving you in control of the supply of coke, meth and girls."

"Why?" He looked like a mathematician who keeps getting five as the answer to two plus two. "It don't make no sense. What are you doing?"

"Just having a beer."

"What are you doing *here*, in Tucson, in Arizona. What the fuck do you want here?"

"Same as the rest of us, pal. Just trying to find a way out of Hell." I turned to Anita again. "Get me a hamburger, will you? I'm starving."

I climbed off the stool and walked over to Arana's table. I pulled out a chair and sat.

"Tell me some more about Rafael Montilla. And the Sinaloa cartel."

"Tell you what?"

"You ever meet him?"

"You kidding me? You gonna go kill *him* now?" He laughed. Juan and Alejandro laughed on cue. I didn't laugh.

"Did you ever meet him?"

"No! I never met him. I buy, I sell, I do what I'm told. I make a lot of money. I live like a fockin' king. But they are the emperors, *amigo*. You should know something. In Mexico, is not the cops that go after the Sinaloa, is the army. They own half of Mexico. *Comprendes?*"

I nodded. I was beginning to. "From Tijuana and Mexicali down to Acapulco."

"You got it. Me? I am dealin' in hundreds of thousands of dollars. Lots of money. But Montilla and Chavez..." He laughed and shook his head. "They are dealin' in billions of dollars. *Thousand of millions!*"

"Like a big, multinational corporation."

"Exactly like that, *amigo*. Now you are beginning to understand."

"Like the pharmaceutical industry."

He spread his hands like I was beginning to get on his nerves. "Enough. I said you got it. No more examples."

But I wasn't talking to him. I was talking to myself, wishing I could talk to Marni. "How can I talk to him? How can I contact him?"

He was shaking his finger at me in a 'no' gesture. "Uh-uh! Uh-uh, *gringo*! No way!"

"I need to talk to him."

"No way!"

"You have some intermediary. Some guy you contact. There must be somebody you talk to."

He pounded his fist on the table. Anita loomed up beside me and placed a burger in a bun on the table. My head was buzzing and I could hear a pounding in my ears. I was physically exhausted, but I was also exhausted from all the killing and all the destruction. I kept repeating to myself that I was in Hell and needed to get out. I said, "How come you knew Emilio?" I picked up the burger and bit into it. I spoke around a mouthful of meat. "Where would you have met him?"

His face was flushed. He looked mad as hell. Juan and Alejandro were sweating and watching each other across the table.

"What, you questioning me now? You askin' *me* questions?"

"You met him when Montilla recruited you." It wasn't a question. It was the only answer that made sense. He went a pasty gray color. "Shit." He stared at me. "I just whacked one of Montilla's *compadres*?"

"I need to talk to him."

"No! *No! You fockin' crazy! Just fockin' go!*"

I picked up the burger with my left hand and bit into it as I reached under my arm with my right. I sat back, chewing, and shot Juan through the eye. Alejando wasn't done gaping when I shot him through the ear. They both sagged in their chairs, goggling at each other across the table, only Juan was also weeping long red tears from his empty left socket. Arana was trembling badly. I swallowed before I spoke.

" You got no gang left, Arana. It's just you and me now. I got to be honest. I'm tired. Real tired. Tired of killing. I'd like it to stop now. But I need you to tell me how you contact Montilla."

He had his hands half raised. "I don't contact Montilla. Nobody contacts Montilla. Montilla contacts you."

That made sense. I took another bite of the burger and spoke with my mouth full. "So who is your contact? Who do *you* talk to?"

His face was pleading. "*Nobody!* The stuff arrives, I distribute to my buyers, everybody gets paid, is cool. You know? No need to talk to nobody."

I sighed. "I don't want to argue with you, Arana. I told you I'm tired. I lost count of how many men I have killed tonight. I want to stop. But I need to know how to contact Montilla, and if you don't tell me I'm going to have to hurt you." He was trembling badly by now. He was sweating and he had tears in his eyes. I wondered how many men he had tortured and killed, how many he had watched beg and plead without showing them compassion. "You don't look to me like a man who would stand up under torture. Don't make me do it."

I stood. He squealed. There was a smell of ammonia on the air. "*No! Wait!*"

"Talk."

"Let me take the money. I'll go. I'll run. Go to India! Or Indonesia! They won't follow me there! I'll tell you everything. Just give me the money and a car! I'll run!"

I nodded. "Deal. Tell me."

He got to his feet and pointed at the stairs. "Is up, in my safe." I waved him on with the Sig. Anita and the other girls were holding each other and weeping silently. I ignored them and followed Arana up a flight of heavy wooden stairs to an oak door. He pushed it open and we went in. The apartment was surprisingly luxurious. We went through a broad living room with a cinema-sized TV and into a den where he had a desk and a computer and a large leather chair. In the corner, like Romero, he had a safe sitting on the floor. He hesitated, turned to look at me.

"You don't need to do this. We can blame Red. We can say he killed my men..."

"I'm going to count to three, then I'm going to shoot you in the elbow."

He waved both hands at me, backed up to the safe and dropped on his knees. He dialed in the combination, then opened the box and pulled out a black book. I stepped behind him. Inside I could see more cash, at least fifty grand. He handed me the book and started pulling out the cash and stacking it on his desk as he spoke.

"Is listed as Control. He told me, never call this number

unless is a life or death situation, you know? No contact, just the deliveries and payment. Everything was workin' like clockwork till you show up, making focking trouble for everybody."

I found the number. The other names all looked like buyers. I shot him while he was kneeling in front of the safe. It seemed appropriate. I went into his bedroom and found a sports bag in his wardrobe. I took it back to his den and piled in the money. It was as I had figured, just over fifty grand. I took it downstairs. Anita was still sitting at the bar with the other two girls. They looked real scared when I came in.

I put the bag on the table next to my rucksack. "You girls legal in this country?"

Anita nodded. "We got papers. You a cop?"

I shook my head and tossed her the sports bag. "Divide it up between you. Get the hell out of here. Get a fucking education. Do something useful that doesn't involve fucking gangsters for a living."

I went back up to the den. I heard the door slam, and a couple of minutes later, the roar of an engine outside and tires on dirt. I grabbed Arana by his heels and dragged him bumping down the stairs. At the bottom, with difficulty, I hoisted him onto my shoulder, carried him out to the Jeep and slung him in the back. By the time I had done the same with Juan and Alejandro, my legs were shaking with exhaustion. I threw Romero's head in for good measure and stuffed the sack of money on the passenger seat.

The cooker at *Casa Coca* was electric, but whiskey and brandy and rum all make pretty good Molotov cocktails. I didn't want my DNA or my fingerprints showing up there when the cops finally came down. But more than that, when

I contacted Montilla, I wanted him to know what Arana discovered just before he died: that I was a destructive son of a bitch who liked to burn things and blow them up.

I had one more thing I had to do that night before I could sleep. I drove north up the 286 till I came to the turnoff for Keystone, where the San Juan county sheriff had his office. It was a fifteen-minute drive into the center of the town. It was a quiet town and by that time, almost one AM, the streets were empty and all the bars were closed. I pulled up outside the county sheriff's office and heaved out Juan's body. I dumped it on the doorstep, then pulled out Alejandro's and threw it on top. I dumped Arana's body on top of Alejandro's and then placed Romero's head on Arana's chest. It made quite a stack.

After that, I climbed into the Jeep and headed for Tucson.

SEVENTEEN

I DUMPED THE JEEP OUTSIDE THE HAWK'S NEST and got in my car. I checked the tracker and my laptop. There was no sign of Marni. I drove back to her house through dull, yellow-lit streets, past quiet houses with blind windows and stationary cars, under a pre-dawn black sky.

Thinking. Or at least, trying to think.

I parked a hundred yards from the house and went the rest of the way on foot, haunted by the echo of my steps. I let myself in and closed the door. The clunk was loud, but the house felt close and silent. I closed the drapes, left the lights off and switched on my laptop.

When my father had first asked me to find Marni, during the summer, he had given me two contacts, people who could help me if I got in trouble. I had never wanted to use them, but I was obsessing now about an idea. There was only one way I could think of to resolve it, and that was through one of those contacts: Philip Gantrie, a brilliant computer nerd who had helped me destroy the Omega sun beetle farm in Colorado.

He had since given me a secure email address. Now I typed him a message.

Need to know all financial investors in University of Arizona School of Natural Resources and the Environment.

The answer came about thirty seconds later:

Will be in touch shortly.

I poured myself a drink and settled to wait.

I woke up to the sound of birds. The room was dark, but there was gray light filtering around the edges of the drapes. My body ached and I had a crick in my neck from the position I'd slept in on the chair. I checked my laptop, but there was still no reply from Phil.

I climbed the stairs, stripped and stood under the shower for ten minutes, turning the water from hot to cold and back again, shocking my body into wakefulness, trying to wash away the carnage of the night. I toweled myself dry and pulled on a clean pair of pants and a T-shirt. Then I reached for my phone. I had six missed calls from Red. I swore under my breath. I must have really been out of it. Not good.

I called him back.

"What the hell have you done to my truck?"

"It's a long story. We were ambushed. I need to see you. Be at the Hawk's Nest in half an hour."

"Hold your fuckin' horses, cowboy. I'm through takin' orders from you. This is *my* operation, you understand me?"

"Just be there."

"I'm already here, Lacklan! Now you get your fuckin' ass over here before I get my bullwhip on you!"

I gave it a beat of three. "If you're going to threaten me, Red, you'd better be ready to make good on it."

"I'm ready."

I hung up, making long movies in my head, trying to play out what had happened during the night and the early morning.

Uncle Caleb had happened. I smiled. He'd found the offering on his doorstep and called Red. Red had gone to the club and found his new Jeep full of blood and gore. Now he wanted to use his bullwhip on me. He was many things, but one thing you could never accuse Red of was being wise.

I made coffee and toast and as I had my breakfast standing in the kitchen I told myself I had to finish this business today. I had been a fool to get involved, but now Arana and Romero were dead, I just needed to deal with Red and his uncle. Case closed.

Arana's supplier was another matter. It was a hell of a coincidence but, if I was right, it led me right back to Marni, which was where I should have been focused all along. I knew Marni had deliberately engineered the situation in Turret, Colorado. But there was no way she could have engineered my meeting Red. That had been pure chance.

I arrived at the Hawk's Nest half an hour later. The sun was high and it was already getting hot. The side of the building was blackened by smoke, but apart from that, and the charred remains of the storage sheds out back, there was not much damage from the fire.

The green Jeep was still there, where I had left it the night before, and the sheriff of San Juan County had his truck parked next to it. There were a couple of other trucks there too. It looked like he had a whole reception committee for me.

I pushed through the door into the dark interior. They were sitting around a table talking, but went silent when I went in. There was Red and there was Chetan, and there were five of their boys. And then there was the Sheriff, standing at the bar. I let the door close and crossed the room to stand looking down at Red.

"Where's your bullwhip, Red?"

"What happened last night?"

"Why don't you ask your uncle, the sheriff of San Juan County?" I looked over at him. "You have a way of straying out of your jurisdiction, don't you, Sheriff?"

"I'm askin' *you*, Lacklan. What the fuck happened last night?"

"What happened was that Arana knew we were coming. When we got to the *Casa Coca* he was waiting for us. He killed your boys, but he tortured us first. Seth told him about Romero being your supplier. He took a gang over the border, took me along to watch. They torched the place, killed everyone and decapitated Romero. He wanted me to tell you what I'd seen. But he made a mistake."

It was the sheriff who asked. His voice was tight. "What mistake?"

I ignored him and kept talking to Red, aware that

Chetan was watching me, still and silent as an iguana. "He chose me to be the messenger. He should have killed me when he had the chance and used Seth instead. When he untied me, I killed him and all his boys, and I torched the *Casa Coca*." Now I turned to the sheriff. "I guess you've seen it by now, huh, Sheriff?"

He nodded, then turned to Red and nodded at him, too. "The place was gutted."

Chetan spoke for the first time. "You want us to believe you killed the whole of Arana's gang?"

"It's easy to kill people when they expect you to do something else, like get on your knees and beg." I turned back to Red. "But you're still asking all the wrong questions. You're stupid and you will always be stupid, right up to the day you get shot between the eyes."

He got to his feet. His face was flushed and his ears were burning. "I've had just about a belly full of you, boy!"

"Are you not wondering? Are you not asking yourself *any* questions?" I bellowed at him suddenly and my voice echoed around the bar. "*How the fuck did Arana know we were coming?*" He stared at me with wide eyes. I kept shouting, driving his simple mind to where I wanted it to be. "*I was with you! I got in the truck with Seth! I was with Seth and the boys all the fucking way down to the Casa Coca! So who the hell told Arana we were coming?*"

Everybody turned their eyes on the sheriff. Everyone except Chetan, who was still watching me. The sheriff went pale and stood away from the bar. "Oh, now wait one goddamn minute!"

I pointed at him. "You were the only person who knew."

"Now that just ain't true! There were any number of people..."

"You want to tell Red about the first time we ever met, Sheriff?"

His face went scarlet. "That don't mean nothin'..."!

Red was glaring at him. "What the hell is goin' on, Uncle Caleb? I thought we had an understanding..."

"We do, son!" He pointed a trembling hand at me. "This feller is a damn trouble-maker! Everywhere he goes, people die, and bad shit happens! You don't want to believe a goddamn thing he tells you!"

"Your uncle was in Arana's pay. He's a gutless piece of shit just like the rest of you. You do with him whatever you think is smart. Arana is not a problem for you anymore. But you *have* got one problem. You no longer have a supplier."

Things were moving too fast for him and he could not keep up. I saw the sheriff frown. He knew I'd let him off the hook and he didn't understand why. Red was trying to catch up with the new topic of conversation, but he was struggling.

"Supplier?"

"Yeah, Red, supplier. Romero is dead. Haven't you been listening, you dumb piece of shit?" I threw Arana's little black book on the table. "Before I killed him, I got the name of Arana's supplier, and his contact number. You want to stay in this business, you're going to have to deal direct with the Sinaloa cartel. A man called Rafael Montilla. You get the product cheaper, but you sell it at the same price. Your profits just went up."

Chetan reached out and picked up the book. He leafed through it with no expression, studying each page. He handed it up to Red, who was frowning hard, like his brain hurt. I went on.

"The number is listed as Control. I just exposed your mole, Red, eliminated your competition and got you the best supplier on the planet. Now, let's talk about that bullwhip..."

He seemed not to hear me. He went through the book and found the number. The sheriff lifted a trembling hand and pointed at me. "Red, now you listen to me, this man is dangerous. I don't know what his game is, but he is turning us against each other, he sows trouble and dissent everywhere he goes. And everywhere he goes, people die. I swear, Red, this man is the fuckin' devil incarnate!"

I snorted. Red looked at me like I'd startled him. I said, "Fix up a meeting. Somewhere in the desert. Tell him both Romero and Arana have been wiped out. You don't know who by, but you've been left without a supplier. Say you want to meet Rafael Montilla in person and you want to deal with him direct. They'll most likely say no, but it's worth asking. This is probably as urgent for them as it is for you. They just lost one of their major supply lines into the USA. See if they'll meet this afternoon or this evening. Call me when it's set up." I gazed at the sheriff and at the five boys at the table. I allowed my contempt to show. "You're going to need somebody who knows what he's doing."

Red was still frowning. "Now...?"

"Yeah, do it now. And, Red, next time you threaten me, I'm going to kill you. Do you understand that?"

Chetan raised an eyebrow. It was the first time I'd ever seen an expression on his face. Maybe I'd gone too far. Maybe I had overstepped the mark. I didn't give a damn.

Maybe I should have.

I left, got into my car and drove the short distance to Cissy's place. It was almost lunchtime by the time I got there. It wasn't the furnace heat of high summer, but it was hot for October. She opened the door to me, sighed and smiled. Then she stepped out, grabbed me and gave me a long, passionate kiss. I was surprised at how good it felt. She eventually pulled back and looked up into my eyes.

"I was beginning to wonder if you'd gone, if I'd ever see you again..."

"Let's go inside, Cissy. I have to talk to you."

"That don't sound good."

I kissed her head and we went inside. She sat at the dining table and I put my rucksack in front of her and opened it. I dumped the money in front of her.

"There's over three hundred grand there, Cissy. I want you to take it and go away for a few days. Things are going to get pretty intense. I want you to be safe."

She was staring at the money, not listening to me. "What the hell have you done, Lacklan? Where did you get this money?"

"That is not important. What is important is how you use it. Red will not bother you again. You'll be free of him by tonight. But I am going to have to move on. I want you to promise me that from now on, you will make smarter choices about the men you let into your life."

She finally looked at me. She was unhappy and shook her head. "I don't like the way you're talking. Why do you have to go?"

"It's complicated to explain, Cissy. I wish I didn't have to, but I do."

I was surprised, again, to discover that I actually meant what I was saying. There was an uncomplicated joy about Cissy. She was what she was, and she found it easy to be happy. You knew with her that if you treated her right she would stand by you to the end. That was all I had ever wanted, yet once again, I found myself walking away from it.

Her eyes flooded. "Why?"

I cupped her cheek in my hand and felt the wetness of her tears, and for a crazy moment I wondered, what if? What if I turned my back on everything and stayed? What if I sent my father and Marni and the whole damn lot of them to the devil, and stayed here with Cissy? Wouldn't that be a way out of Hell?

I kissed her. "We'll talk. Right now I have to go. I want you to take the money and disappear for a couple of days. When you get back, it'll be over and we'll talk. I promise."

I left her in the kitchen, drying her eyes and looking at the blood-stained money on the table, like it was something she had just stepped in on the sidewalk.

EIGHTEEN

I CLIMBED INTO MY CAR, LIT A PUEBLO AND started to drive, not knowing exactly where I was going. My phone pinged to tell me I had an email. I thumbed the screen while I drove and saw it was from Phil. I pulled onto a patch of wasteland and opened the message.

ARE YOU ALONE? Can I call you?

I ANSWERED:

YES.

A FEW SECONDS later my phone rang.

"Don't use names. This is a secure line, but it pays to be careful."

"Hi."

"I looked into your request. I'll send you a bill and method of payment separately. The School of Natural Resources and the Environment has a large number of donors. They are like investors in that they, directly or indirectly, derive benefits from the research one way or another. They range from the government and environmental pressure groups to private industry. I'm going to email you the complete list so you can look at it."

"Thanks, did any particular investors stand out..."

"Try not to talk. I'm coming to that. There are a few who stand out for a couple of reasons. The first reason is that they actually have a stake in the results of the research."

"A stake in what sense?"

"In the sense that they partially own the results."

I thought about that for a moment. "Who?"

"Wait. So, these investors are actually investing not so much in the faculty as a whole, but in a particular project."

"Like what?"

"Stop interrupting and listen to me. There are three projects in particular, and they are all directly or indirectly overseen by one professor. They are the Biosphere 3 Project, in construction at Buena Vista Lake, south of Beyerville."

"On the Santa Cruz river..."

"Yes. Ostensibly, its main function will be to research insect life and its potential in regenerating desert ecosystems."

I was only half listening. My mind was racing. The Santa Cruz River was the river that ran through Romero's ranch.

It meant something, but I could not see it yet. Phil was still talking.

"The second is Project Apollo, nothing to do with rockets, and it is a bit bizarre that they should be conducting this research in that particular faculty, as it belongs more to neurosciences. What they are doing is growing brains—human brains—like they were cabbages or something, on other animals, like rats."

"*What?*"

"I'm serious. The plan is to see if certain neural functions can be transferred to other organisms to assist in regenerating dead earth. Kind of imbuing an ecosphere with intelligence."

"Jesus Christ..."

"You're not kidding. That is the declared purpose, I'm willing to bet they are also researching ways to manipulate those brains—a kind of neural biofeedback from the environment. The third project is called Social Environmentalism. It hooks up with the departments of Social Sciences and Psychology to study the interaction of the environment with the collective human psyche. Two large investors stood out who put a lot of money into all three of these projects, and bought proprietary rights in all of them."

"Who?"

"Inversiones Sonora, based in Hermosillo, in Mexico. Phoenix Investments, based in DC, and R&D Funding, based in Boston. I dug a little further to see if any significant names showed up on the boards. You know I can get access to lists that are confidential and hidden to other people."

"Yeah, what did you find?"

"Well, to begin with, Phoenix Investments and R&D

Funding both belong to a company called Globex, which is registered in Switzerland. And Globex belongs to the Maya Corporation, based in Belize. And the main shareholder in the Maya Corporation, as you have probably guessed…"

"Is Inversiones Sonora."

"You guessed."

"So basically these three projects are being funded by, and belong to, Inversiones Sonora."

"Correct, and Inversiones Sonora is, being very simplistic, a huge money laundering scheme for…"

"The Sinaloa cartel."

He was silent for a moment. "Yeah, I guess I told you what you expected me to tell you."

"Yes, but a lot more than that too. What about people?"

"Three names stand out as being involved in the projects as financial directors. Rafael Montilla for Sonora, William George Codey, a Congressman, for Phoenix Investments, and Roman Paglieri for R&D Funding. There is one senior professor at the university who is involved as a director of research in all three projects."

I went cold and felt my hair prickle on my head. "Engels…"

"Yeah."

"Shit."

"Not good news, huh?"

"No, not good news."

"Hope you sort it, dude. Bill's in the post, metaphorically."

He hung up and I sat staring at the burning tip of my cigarette. For a moment it looked like a burning globe, a scorched planet, a dying world.

It was too big, too vast to comprehend. My head was reeling. I needed to know where Marni had gone. I needed to talk to her. For a moment, I thought about going to the university and abducting Engels' secretary and beating their whereabouts out of her. But I knew that would not lead anywhere good. All I could do was wait for them to get back.

And hope that she did get back.

I drove the rest of the way to the house through the afternoon sun, left the car down the road, where she wouldn't see it when she finally came home, and let myself in. It was still silent and dead. I threw myself on the sofa to stare at the ceiling and wait, either for Marni to come back or Red to call and tell me he'd fixed up a meeting with Montilla, or one of his representatives.

I kept getting waves of anger at Marni. Why was she so damn obstinate? Why would she not confide in me? Why did she not trust me? What was it she kept saying? Do your reading. And while she sent me off to do my reading, like some misbehaved school kid, she cozied up with some son of a bitch who was in the pay of the biggest drugs cartel in the world. Smart move, Marni.

Do your reading.

I swung off the couch and went upstairs. I rummaged in my drawer and found the diary she had left for me, back when I'd tracked her to the old hideout we used to use when we were kids on holiday in Turret, Colorado. It was the only thing she could be referring to when she told me to 'do my reading'.

Why would she want me to read her diary? It was not even current. It was years old, from shortly after she'd gradu-ated, while she was doing her doctoral thesis. I carried it downstairs and dropped on the sofa again, started leafing through it. A lot of it was just reflections about her research and comments about colleagues. As I read, I could hear her voice in my mind, maturing from the passionate, naïve girl to the equally passionate, focused woman. She talked about her growing awareness of her father's work. She talked about the fact that he had blazed the trail for her, but she didn't mention how. She talked about his research, but said that there were important notes and documents missing. Vital documents that she needed, and she wondered what he had done with them.

There were other passages where she spoke with love and respect about my father, Robert. She had trusted him and relied on him. He had been a surrogate father for her, until she had discovered—until I had told her—that he had killed her true father.

I turned page after page, searching. What was it she wanted me to read here? What was it I was supposed to find? Perhaps nothing. Perhaps just as she had killed Robert, she now wanted to eliminate me from her life, too. Perhaps the associations were too awful. Perhaps she had grown to hate me.

But my mind went around and around in circles. If she hated me, if she wanted to eliminate me from her life, then why had she made herself, and her plates, so visible at the funeral? She knew what I was like. She knew that would be enough to bring me to Tucson. So what the hell was she playing at? Why, 'Go home, do your reading'? Why those particular words?

Unless...

I began to look at it from a different angle. I closed my

eyes and visualized the ad she'd put in the paper for me. *'Kyle Rees, you have seen what you came to see. Now go home. Do your reading.'*

How did she know what I had seen? She hadn't even known I was in Tucson. The only things she knew I had seen were her and her plates. As far as she was concerned when she wrote that ad, I was still in Boston. So how could I 'go home' if I was already home? She had called me Kyle Rees. Kyle Rees had come from the future to protect Sarah Connor. She had called herself Sarah Connors on the car registration, which she had known I would find.

I sat up. So she was acknowledging that I was there to protect her. She was not rejecting me. Therefore, when she referred to 'home' what was she talking about? Back to the beginning? To square one? Back to base? Turret? Our hideout?

Go back to what I had found in our hideout and read it. Why? Apart from suggesting that she was not rejecting me, it got me nowhere.

My cell rang and I grabbed it. It was Red.

"It's set up for tonight. Come to the Nest. Now."

He didn't wait for me to answer. He just hung up.

I smoked another cigarette and thought. Then I stepped out and walked to my car. I had a bad feeling. It was a very bad feeling. I knew things were about to get real ugly, but there was nothing I could do about it except meet the ugliness head on, and fight.

I drove through the gathering dusk, in the fading light of the dying sun, and eventually pulled onto the dusty forecourt of the Hawk's Nest. The green Jeep had gone, but the other trucks were still there, though their position had changed. They had left and come back. My gut was telling me this was bad, but I could not yet tell why.

I climbed out of the car and walked to the door. It said it was closed, but I pushed in anyway. I took a couple of steps and heard the door thud closed behind me. Red was where he had been, sitting at the table. His boys were sitting around him. The sheriff was behind the bar getting himself a beer. I couldn't see Chetan, but I knew he was behind me. I knew he was behind me because Cissy was sitting at the table. Her eyes were puffy from crying. My rucksack was there too, with all the money spilled out across the table.

Only Chetan, I told myself, out of this bunch of mental retards, had the brains to work out there was something between me and Cissy, and follow me when I'd left.

I felt the muzzle of his revolver in the back of my neck, and heard the click of the hammer. That was twice, I told myself. Twice since following Marni to Tucson that I had been stupid and careless. And both times had been because of sentimentality over Cissy. There could not be a third time. The third time would cost one of us our life.

Chetan spoke softly in my ear. "You ain't playing with stupid kids anymore. I'm onto you. Sneeze in a way I don't like and I will cut her into small pieces and feed her to you. You understand me?"

"What do you want?"

Red grinned. "It ain't so much what *we* want, Lacklan. It's what our new best friend Rafael wants. And he wants you. But before we hand you over, we want to have a little fun. Sit down while I tell you what's going to happen next."

NINETEEN

It was like a hammer blow, just above my kidneys and into my lower ribs, knocking all the air out of my lungs and sending shards of crippling pain through my chest, sapping the strength from my legs and my arms. Next came the kick to the back of my knee, and I went crashing between the chairs against the table.

I braced myself for the barrage of kicks and stamps that I assumed was coming next. But instead, Red's boys got up from the table, and while Chetan covered me, they took my Sig and my knife. I could hear Cissy screaming at Red to stop. There was a loud slap, I heard her gasp and then she was silent. I raised my head and saw her blinking away tears. She looked stunned. I mouthed at her, "*Shut up!*" Then I looked for Red.

He'd moved to the far end of the room and was now returning. He had a long coil of rope in his hands. The sheriff loomed up beside me and clapped his cuffs on my wrists. Next thing Red was looping the rope though the cuffs and tossing it up over one of the rafters. Then he and a couple of his boys heaved and dragged until I was hanging about an inch off the floor.

If you've never been hung like that, you have no idea how painful it is. Pretty soon all your back muscles and your intercostals start to go into spasm, you can't breathe and you start to suffocate. The worst thing is, the harder you try to fight it, the more severe the spasms become. The only thing you can do is try to relax your breathing and go limp. Which is not easy when you have eight guys looking at you, whose main purpose in life is to cause you as much pain as they can.

Red spoke first.

"You been screwing my girl."

I shook my head. "I tried, but she wasn't interested."

The backhand was fast, and Red was as strong as he was stupid. My head rang like a bell and I heard Chetan's voice, low and ruthless, saying, "Don't kill him. We need him for Montilla."

"Tell me the truth."

"That is the truth, you fucking asshole. Why do you think I moved out?"

"Why'd you give her the money?"

I snarled at him. "I'm not as stupid as you look, Red! I didn't give her the fucking money. I stashed it in my room while I checked out the new place and found somewhere to hide it."

It was a desperate lie, and it sounded desperate. I could see Chetan smiling. Only the second time I'd seen an expression on his face. He was examining my knife.

"I could almost believe you. You lie with real skill. That makes you very dangerous, Lacklan. A man must be very careful with somebody like you. And that's why I followed you when you left. If you are not screwing Red's girl, and you did not give her the money, maybe you can explain why we saw you kissing in the doorway."

I sighed. "I forced her..."

He continued in his relentless, monotonous voice. "Now you are making stupid mistakes, Lacklan. We saw clearly that *she* kissed you. But you are ready to risk your life to protect her. That means you have feelings for her. That means we have you. We have real power over you."

I looked at his bland, smiling face and knew that I had badly underestimated him. Sheriff Caleb stepped into view with his thumbs in his belt. He stood up close and stared into my face. "Who are you?"

I held his eye. "The man who's going to kill you."

It was stupid and it earned me another backhand, but it made me feel better. I was disoriented, but the taste of blood helped to focus my mind.

"I'm going to ask you again, boy. Who are you and what are you doing here?"

The truth was more improbable than any lie I could dream up. I toyed with the idea of telling him I was CIA. I'd got as far as wondering how they'd check that and how I could confirm it, when suddenly, out of the blue and for no apparent reason, Red started whaling into me with his fists, snarling and spitting, pounding my ribs and my face. The pain was excruciating. They train you to deal with this kind of thing in the Regiment, but it never gets easy. All you can do is withdraw inside, go with the pain and promise yourself vengeance when the time comes.

I felt my lip swelling and tried to keep my eyes away from

his fists. When that time came, I wanted to be able to see him; to see his face.

Chetan and the sheriff dragged him away. His cheeks were crimson and he was screaming, "*You think you can come here, screwing my woman, takin' my money, you mother fucker!*"

Chetan held up my Fairbairn & Sykes. "This is a military knife. Its used by the British Commandos. Your piece, Sig Saur p226 Tacops. That's an expensive gun. Also used by the military." He pointed at me. "You are military. Now I'm going to ask you one more time nicely, and after that it's going to get bad. Who are you and what are you doing here?"

I closed my eyes and sighed. It was genuine. Right then, I was all out of options. I told the most convincing lie I could think of, because they would never believe the truth.

"I'm special ops. I'm here on an assignment that does not concern you. Like a damn fool, I fell for Cissy and got dragged into this bullshit."

Chetan frowned at the blade of the knife. "Special ops? What the hell is a special ops operative doing in Arizona? Shouldn't you be in Iraq or Afghanistan?"

"You're way out of date, pal. The enemy isn't overseas anymore. It's right here at home."

He gave a rueful snort. "Ain't that the truth." But then he got that constipated look and spread his hands. "But all this? Arana, Romero... What was that? In your spare time while on another assignment?" He shook his head. "That's bullshit and you know it."

Put like that, I kind of agreed with him, but it was also kind of true. I sighed again. "Think of me as Superman, truth and justice, the American way." I jerked my head at Red. "I saw this son of a bitch beating up on his girl, and it made me mad. When I get mad, I have no sense of proportion."

Red was staring at his pal. "You believe this shit?"

The sheriff said, "He ain't a Fed, that's for sure. And he ain't from the Arizona PD."

Chetan gave a single nod. "He's military. He ain't law enforcement. He's either acting solo or his story is true."

Red walked up and stood bending his knees and adjusting his shoulders, like his skin didn't fit. "So, what happens now, Mr. Special Ops? We hand you over to Montilla, he's gonna gut you like a fish. What happens then?"

"You serious, Red? Have a look around. What do you think is going to happen when my team comes looking for me?"

Chetan chuckled and stood. "The military don't avenge their own. That ain't how it works. You sign up, you know the score. Especially special ops. Either way, we hand him over to Montilla and it's the Sinaloa's problem, not ours."

Red shook his head. "That's it?"

Chetan stood close to him, so they were almost touching. "We don't give a shit what his story is, Red. We only care about what it ain't. He ain't after us. He ain't interested in us. Whatever he was sent here for, it was not you and me. His beef with us was personal. So we give him to Montilla and wash our hands."

Red's voice was almost hysterical. "And what about me? I'm entitled to me revenge. Eye for an eye..."

Chetan's voice dropped to a rasp. "You get that when we hand him over to the Sinaloa."

The sheriff broke in, sounding reasonable. "Get a grip, Red. Don't show yourself up in front of your boys." Red and Chetan stared each other down for a count of five, then Red said, "Cut him down."

Two boys cut the rope. I tried to stand but my legs buckled and I sprawled on the floor. A powerful hand grabbed the scruff of my neck and dragged me to my feet. Then they took my arms, pulled me stumbling across the bar and out the door into the parking lot. There was no moon, the stars were pinpricks of cold light in a black sheet of emptiness. And from where we stood, on the edge of the desert, Tucson was a glow on the horizon, that right then seemed very far away.

The sheriff slapped Red on his shoulder. "I can't be a part of this. I'll catch you later. Let me know how it goes."

He crossed the lot, climbed in his truck, and drove away into the night. When he'd gone, Red came up close to me and grabbed my face in his hand. There was madness in his eyes, like a kind of frenzy. "You're going to hell, boy. Tonight, you are going to hell."

They bundled me in the back of an SUV with a baboon on either side. All around me doors slammed like a fusillade. The engines roared, the tires kicked up dirt, and we were away. I didn't see where Cissy was, or even if they'd brought her, but I was guessing they had her in a truck behind us. I was also pretty sure that tonight was not going to end well for either one of us. There was death in the air. Death and madness. You could smell it.

We drove fast, in convoy, plunging west through the

desert. At first I thought we were headed for Three Points, and we were going back to Mexico through Abasse. But we hit Three Points and kept on going on the Ajo Highway. We kept going for an hour, till we came to Sells. At Sells, we turned south onto Route 19. The lights of the town died away behind us and we plunged on, deeper into the darkness.

Somewhere inside I was aware that I might be afraid. I was aware I could well die that night. I would almost certainly be tortured. And they had Cissy. As long as they had Cissy, I was powerless.

I was also aware that I was no longer dealing with saps like Red. Chetan was smart, and Montilla was going to be real smart. I was in trouble, and right to be scared. I had lost control of the game, and I was going down fast.

We drove for fifteen minutes, crossed through the scattered cluster of houses that was the village of Topawa, and kept going south. I began to think maybe we were going to cross the border. Maybe we were going into Mexico.

But we weren't. After another fifteen minutes, we arrived at a scattering of shacks and buildings gathered around a small gas station. We turned right off the 19 and onto a dirt track. There were no roads or streets here, just beaten paths between ramshackle buildings. We came to a halt outside an old, whitewashed church. The pale walls looked almost blue in the starlight.

Chetan spoke for the first time since we'd left the club. "This is the old mission of San Patricio. The white government here stole our country, put us on reservations, like rare animals, like they were doing us a favor. Now they neglect us so that we live in ghettos on our own land. But Montilla and

Chavez, through the Sinaloa, they help their people. In Mexico they build schools, hospitals and affordable housing. They help the poor, they help people get back on their feet when they have been robbed and exploited by the multinationals.

"Now they are going to help us here. Soon the people of San Patricio will have business projects, maybe a casino, a hotel, opportunities..." He turned in his seat to look at me. "What do you think, white man? You think we should trust you instead of him?"

I raised an eyebrow at him. "White man?" I jerked my head at Red. "Who's he, Sitting Bull?"

He leered at me and turned to look out of the windshield again. Out of the darkness in the south, an intense light appeared, seemed to warp and separate, like a crazy dividing cell, then resolved itself into a column of headlamps headed our way.

I felt sick. Things were about to get ugly.

TWENTY

THERE WERE THREE DARK BLUE AUDIS. THEY approached at a sedate pace, came off the road making small plumes of dust, and pulled up in front of the mission church. The doors opened almost simultaneously and ten men got out. They were all dressed in dark suits and they all had long, dark blue coats. It was like a scene from Men in Black.

Chetan said, "Come on," and he and Red climbed out of the SUV. He leaned in the back window and stared at me and my two guards with his dark, expressionless face. "You stay till I tell you to get out."

More car doors slammed behind us and I watched Red and Chetan with their boys approach the men in suits. There was a lot of smiling and hand-shaking. It might have been a regular business meeting in Manhattan, only we were in the most remote part of the Sonora Desert in Arizona, at night, and they were trading my life for a cocaine concession.

It wasn't hard to identify Montilla. His manner was more reserved than the others. He smiled less, and when he spoke, everybody looked and listened. He was bald on top, but he'd let the band of hair at the back of his head grow long, and I noticed that his shoes, instead of high polish patent leather, were sneakers. An eccentric. Eccentrics are dangerous, because they are hard to predict.

He said something, made a gesture toward the church and he and his men in suits started moving that way, while Red and Chetan came back towards the trucks, gesturing for us to get out.

The baboon on my right gave me a shove. "OK, boy, git!" The guy on my left climbed out, grabbed hold of me with both hands and heaved. I was feeling pretty weak from the beating, but I put on a show of being all but finished and fell to the dirt. He gave me a couple of kicks that didn't really hurt and dragged me to my feet. Then they were shoving me past the cars toward the church. I saw they had the doors open and a light had come on inside, casting a depressing, yellow glow on the dust. Behind me, I heard Cissy's voice cry out, as though she'd been pushed or hit. I forced myself not to look, not to react. However hard it was, I had to convince them somehow I didn't give a damn about her.

The church was of a simple design. The walls were white. The benches were crudely made from wood. There was a small altar at the end, dominated by a huge crucifix, a few painted plaster saints, and a virgin, who all looked real sad.

The lights came from plastic candles that had been screwed into a couple of wagon wheels suspended from the rafters above. There were real church candles around the altar, and the guy I assumed was Montilla walked toward them, with his rubber soles squeaking loudly on the terracotta floor. He pointed at the candles and said, "*Enciendan las velas.*" A couple of his boys went over and started lighting them. My feeling of sick apprehension grew deeper.

He turned and seemed to study me for a moment. I spoke first.

"Are you Rafael Montilla?"

The question seemed to amuse him. "You think I am Mexican?"

"I don't give a damn whether you're Mexican. I asked if you are Rafael Montilla."

"I am not Mexican. I am Spanish." He pronounced it like it had an 'E' in front, 'Espanish.'

"Is that supposed to mean something to me?"

He creased up his eyes and kind of wheezed and giggled. He gestured with his hand and said, "*Sujétenlo.*"

A couple of his guys pushed Red's men aside and grabbed my arms. He strolled over to me and looked up into my face. He had large, intelligent eyes, but all I could read in them was that he was obsessed with his own power and position.

"You have a choice here today, Lacklan." He shrugged, talking with his body the way Mediterraneans do. "Is always the same choice in life. To suffer or not to suffer."

"You're going to torture and kill me, Montilla, don't make me listen to your undergraduate philosophy as well."

There was a flicker of irritation, but it was soon replaced again by the wheezing giggle. "Cooperate with me an' I kill you quick an' the girl goes free. Don't cooperate an' I torture you both an' you both die." He pulled up his shoulders and pulled down the corners of his mouth. "Is no complicated, I think."

"It's not complicated, Montilla. It's simple. Every word out of your mouth is worth shit. So give me one reason to believe you might be telling the truth, and I might cooperate."

He got that same smug expression on his face that Socrates must have had every time he led some bozo into seeing his own stupidity. "Certainty of suffering for you an' the girl, versus, possibility of no suffering..." He spread his hands.

I nodded. "Oh, I see. So how can I cooperate?"

He paused, examining my expression, trying to work out if it was irony he was seeing in my face. "Who do you work for?"

"Myself."

He was very fast. He was skilled in martial arts. His fist flashed from his hip and plunged deep into my floating ribs. The pain was deep and drained all the blood from my head, making me go dizzy. I felt nauseous and my legs gave under me. I heard him say, "*Llévenlo al altar.*" They dragged me down the central aisle and up the two stone steps onto the altar. There they dumped me on the floor and he stood over me. "*Traigan a la chica.*"

Bring the girl. They dragged her up in front of me. She was struggling and shouting at them to let her go. I refused to look at her. I looked at Montilla instead and tried to convince myself I would kill him that night.

"It's the truth, you asshole. You want me to tell you a lie that you want to hear, or you want the truth?"

He shook his head. "Is not credible."

"What do you want me to say? I work for the CIA? OK! I work for the CIA. Now what?"

He pointed at me and snapped, "*Las muñecas!*"

Now I saw that one of the guys had a coil of rope. They grabbed me between four of them and tied the rope around my left wrist. I shouted at him. "*What the fuck do you want! I'm willing to cooperate!*"

"Who do you work for?"

"*Myself!*"

They dragged me backward toward the crucifix and threw the rope over the left arm of the cross. Another guy started tying a second rope to my right wrist. They were going to crucify me, literally.

Montilla's voice was dull and monotonous. "What are you doing in Tucson?"

My mind was racing. I needed to play for time and I needed to avoid getting strung up on the cross. Once I was up there, I knew I would be powerless.

"I was searching for somebody."

He glanced at his boys and they paused. My right wrist was bound, but he hadn't thrown the rope over the arm yet.

"Who were you searching for?"

My heart was pounding. I spoke carefully. "A woman. She has nothing to do with your operation. She is a girl I knew when I was young. We were in love." He raised an eyebrow like he was losing patience. I rushed on, "Just listen to me, would you! I'm telling you the truth. "She wanted us to marry. I was in the SAS—the British special ops regiment. I figured it was no life for her and I told her no."

"You were in the SAS?"

"Ten years."

That made sense to him and he nodded. "Who is this woman?"

I sighed. "She was my childhood sweetheart. We grew up together. My dad died a couple of months ago. I inherited a lot of money. She didn't want to see me anymore and she came out to Arizona. I followed her here and wanted to convince her we could try again. But she wouldn't see me."

He was shaking his head, but I could tell by his eyes he was half convinced. "This is bullshit."

"No, it's not. I'm telling you the truth. I lodged with Cissy. First night I was there this piece of shit..." I jerked my head at Red. "...beat her up. I felt sorry for her, but she told me what a great guy he was and begged me not to hurt him. I guess stupidity is a female condition."

I put more feeling into the words than I had expected, and it must have sounded believable. I saw him hesitate and glance at Cissy. Red looked confused, too. Montilla said, "So?"

"So I decided to have a private chat with Red. I was going to break his fingers and tell him to lay off Cissy. I like her. She's a sweet kid. I'm not crazy about her, but she's sweet and she doesn't deserve to get beaten up by this chicken-shit redneck. While I was at his club, I saw he was trading coke and whores, and I decided, while I was looking for Sarah..."

He leapt on it like a snake. "Sarah?"

I hesitated, like I'd made a mistake. "My girl. While I

looked for her, I'd do the world a favor and screw up his operation. One thing led to another and here I am... That is the story."

He stared at me a long time. He was smart and he could sense there was truth in what I was saying, but he could also sense there was more to the story than I was telling him. Finally he said, "Maybe."

"Maybe? What are you talking about, *maybe?*"

He jerked his head and snapped, "*Álcenlo!*"

The guy on my right threw the rope over the cross and they both started to pull. I have experienced a lot of pain in my life. I have never experienced anything comparable to those few seconds as I was being dragged up that cross. It was a pain that cannot be described. To say that it was like having long shards of glass driven through my lungs does not begin to describe it. My lungs contracted and all the muscles in my back and my chest, trying to hold the weight of my body, went into spasm, so I could not breathe or shout or cry out to release the agony in my chest. After four or five heaves on the rope, when my own body was covering that of Jesus behind me, I managed to find a foothold on his feet, and the nail that was driven through them. And so I found some small relief for my arms and lungs.

I was aware of a voice screaming and crying, and slowly realized it was Cissy, begging them to let me down. Montilla was smiling up at me.

"It looks as if the girl has stronger feelings for you than you for her, Lacklan."

I rasped, "Don't be stupid, you fucking psychopath. That is a normal, decent, human reaction to torture, you stupid motherfucker! Let her go, she has no part in this."

He cocked his head on one side and shrugged. "Maybe so and maybe not, and in the end, the most likely thing is, who knows?"

He turned and swept everything off the altar. There was a clattering of gold and brass and silver on the stone steps. His voice rang out, like he was giving a sermon. "Are you a Christian, Lacklan?" He waited for an answer, but every word was agony, and I knew that whatever I said would make no difference. He went on, "I am an atheist. Gods, temples, religions—mind control for powerful men to take possession of the brains and emotions of the sheep."

I moaned, "More fucking undergraduate philosophy."

He gestured with his chin at the altar. "*Pónganla en el altar. Átenla.*"

Four of them grabbed Cissy and dragged her kicking and screaming to the altar. They lifted her onto it and pinned her down while a fifth guy tied her ankles and her wrists so that she was splayed helpless across the top.

Montilla pointed at her and looked up at me. "This, this is the ritual that counts. This is the ritual that has meaning. When one man sacrifices the lives of another man and a woman to increase his own power. Now I am sending a strong message to everybody in this room, that I have no limitations in what I will do to get, and hold onto, temporal power."

I curled my lip and snarled, "You have no power over me, Montilla."

He looked genuinely surprised and laughed out loud. "Are you serious?"

"Even if I gave a damn at this stage about the woman, I know that whatever I do and whatever I say, the outcome will be the same. You are going to kill us both. Once you made that clear, you lost your power over me. You set me free, pal. Stick that in your philosophical pipe and smoke it, asshole."

He nodded, smiling. "Maybe." Still smiling at me, he said, "*Traigan la navaja.*"

Bring the knife.

TWENTY-ONE

Cᴜssʏ ʜᴀᴅ ɢᴏɴᴇ ᴀ ʜᴏʀʀɪʙʟᴇ, ᴘᴀsᴛʏ ᴡʜɪᴛᴇ ᴄᴏʟᴏʀ and was trembling uncontrollably. Her eyes, wide with terror, were fixed on my face, like she was expecting me to do something. There was a bustle of movement among Montilla's suits and one of them produced a long, slim-bladed dagger. He handed it to Montilla, who went over and stood looking down at Cissy's face.

The pain in my chest was spreading to my back and had become unendurable. But I kept asking myself, once it became unendurable, what then? I still had to go through it. But I could feel my mind slipping, like I was beginning to hallucinate. I fought to keep control, but when I spoke, my voice came out like a raw rasp.

"What do I need to do to convince you that she is no part of this? What do I need to do to convince you I am telling you the truth?"

He shrugged. "I am not sure. I am not sure you actually can convince me. For now I am planning on removing her fingers one by one, at the joint. We see how you react, if you change your story, if you offer me some proof..." He frowned. "What is this Sarah's full name?"

"Sarah Connors..."

He laughed out loud. "Seriously? Like the Terminator? *Seriously?*"

I snarled at him and shouted, "*No! Not like the damn Terminator! Connors! Not Connor, Connors!*"

He raised an eyebrow. "Address?"

A dim light arose in my mind. I couldn't see it clearly yet, but it was there, glimmering. Maybe, just maybe...

"I hadn't got that far yet. But I know she was seeing a guy at the university."

He trailed the blade across Cissy's belly, slowly moving down. She shuddered and made a horrible, guttural noise.

"I think you are bullshitting me, Lacklan. That is a very dangerous thing to do."

"You're wrong. His name is Engels. You can Google him. He's a professor at the School of Natural Resources and the Environment..."

He had frozen long before I reached the end of the sentence. He stood for a long moment staring at nothing. Finally, he said, "What is your surname, Lacklan?"

"Walker."

He turned to look up at me, like the name was vaguely familiar. "Lacklan Walker..."

I gave my voice no particular inflection. "That name familiar to you?"

"Who is your father?"

"Cut her loose. I keep telling you she is no part of this."

Red was scowling at Montilla. "What the hell is going on now?"

"What is the name of your father?" His voice had an edge to it.

I half-shouted, "It is who you think it is, Montilla! Robert Walker! Gamma! That mean anything to you? I know about your investment in the Biosphere, in Project Apollo and the Social Environmentalism Project! Now, you want to talk, let's talk, but let the girl go, for fuck's sake! She is *not* a part of this!"

Red had gone puce and his eyes were shining with growing anger. "What the hell is going on here?"

Chetan was shaking his head and pulling at Red's arm. "We don't want to be a part of this..."

Montilla drew breath, paused, then closed his mouth and held out his hand. "*Teléfono!*"

A suit handed him a cell and he walked down the central aisle punching in a number. Now the game had shifted. As I had hoped, he had lost interest in Cissy. Instead, I had probably signed my own death warrant. But there was a chance, a slim chance, I could talk my way out. It was a slim chance, but it was also the only chance I had.

I looked down at Cissy. She looked as though she'd gone into shock, her eyes locked on mine, wide and staring. My head was foggy and I felt I was losing consciousness. I forced myself to focus on Red and Chetan. They were speaking urgently to each other in muted voices. Their guys looked uncomfortable and scared. The suits looked impassive. They knew somebody was going to die tonight, but they didn't care who. I spoke up, and my voice sounded half-dead in my own ears.

"Things are getting away from you, Chetan." I gave an ugly laugh. "You can feel it, can't you? This is one of those situations where nobody gets out alive." They all frowned at me. I shifted my eyes to his boys. "If I were you, I'd be making for the cars before it's too late."

The suits were glancing at each other and smiling. They knew what I was doing and they thought it was funny. They thought they were in control. They didn't understand that I was teasing that control out of their fingers.

My feet were beginning to slip off the nail in Jesus' foot. Exhaustion was taking a hold of me, and I knew that I had to do something fast or it would be too late. I said, "You know what we have here, don't you, Chetan?" I tried to study his face, though my eyes were losing focus with the pain and the lack of air. "What we have here is unwelcome witnesses. You and Red and the boys, are all becoming witnesses to something you were not supposed to be privy to..."

Montilla's suits had stopped smiling and had that 'uh-oh' look on their faces. One of them spoke for the first time and said, "*Calla la boca ya, gringo!*"

I gave a small, humorless laugh. It hurt.

"You speak Spanish, don't you, Chetan? Why do you think he's telling me to shut up?" I gave another, weary laugh, even though it still hurt from last time. "Why do you think they were so interested in getting a hold of me? You are so out of your depths here, boys. There is going to be a lot of killing tonight..."

"*Que te calles ya! Cojones!*"

Which basically meant 'shut the fuck up'.

I heard Montilla's rubber soles squeaking back along the

central aisle. He stopped and stood looking up at me, like a man questioning his own faith.

"I don't know what you hoped to achieve, Lacklan. I guess it was a desperate, last ditch attempt, huh? Now I know who you are, I don' need you no more. Time to die."

"What about the girl?"

He smiled. "Seriously?"

"You can't leave witnesses, right?"

His right-hand suit turned to give him a warning look just a little too late. Montilla had opened his mouth to answer, but Chetan, Red and his boys had all drawn their weapons. Red's voice was high and shrill.

"I don't know what the fuck is going on here, but we are gonna walk out, git in our trucks and leave you to do whatever the fuck it is you are plannin' on doing."

Montilla held up his hands as his own boys pulled their weapons. Red was outnumbered, but not by much, and Montilla had to be aware that in a shoot out in the open church, he was seriously at risk.

"Take it easy, guys, you got the wrong end of the stick. We are partners. We are on the same side, right?"

"Are we?" It was Chetan. "What's all this shit about his name and Gamma and the university?" He shook his head. "Don't tell me. We don't wanna know. We just want out of here, and leave you to play whatever fuckin' games you're playing with this motherfucker."

Montilla's face had gone deadly. His voice was real quiet. "What's the hurry? We have business to discuss. You are our guests." He gave a small laugh that was as cold as a dead hand. "You're the guests of the Sinaloa. We are going to eat an' drink, an' talk business..."

I tried to laugh, but it came out as a cackle. "Punks to push his dope are a dime a dozen on any fucking street corner from San Diego to Miami. But people who know about Omega and Gamma, they are a fucking risk to your masters, isn't that so, Montilla?"

"Shut the fuck up, Lacklan. You want your lady to get out of here alive today, you better shut the fuck up."

I laughed out loud, like a madman, even though the pain was excruciating. "Too late, Montilla! Too late, Chetan! None of us can leave here alive tonight! Omega cannot allow it! You have got to kill us all, now, Montilla! You have to kill us all, and you know it!"

I don't know who realized it first. It was a matter of microseconds. But both Chetan and Montilla got it. There was no way that situation was going to end without blood-shed. Whoever got off the first round had the edge.

As Chetan screamed, "*Kill the motherfuckers!*" Montilla was screaming, "*Mátenlos! Mátenlos a todos!*"

Then all hell broke loose. Red and Chetan and his boys were backing into the pews, taking cover behind the stone pillars that held up the arches and the roof. Montilla and his men were doing the same thing, amid a hail of bullets across the central aisle. At the same time, both sides were edging toward the door. Red and Chetan to escape, Montilla to cut them off and kill them. But all I could see was that with about twenty rounds going off every second, the chances of a ricochet hitting Cissy, who was screaming hysterically, were getting higher at every moment.

Fear, pain, and despair can give a man almost super-human strength. As the shooting started, and I heard Cissy's panic as she screamed, my belly flooded with burning adrenaline and I pulled in a kind of frenzy, flattening my hands against the wood. I screamed at the top of my lungs and the agony in my back and my chest sent my muscles into a kind of seizure. I felt the skin rip from my wrists and blood flood my hands as I pulled, and suddenly, I was falling, dropping to the floor.

I landed in a heap at the bottom of the cross. My breath was coming in gasps that I couldn't control, but I clawed my way across the floor toward the altar. I reached out and grabbed one of the tall, wrought iron candlesticks and pulled it toward me. It tipped over and the thick church candle fell by my face. I took it and put the flame against the rope that held Cissy, dousing it in wax to make it burn faster. It caught and I seized hold of it with both my torn, bloodied hands and pulled. It snapped and I reached up for Cissy, pulling her down from the altar on top of me in a heap. She clung to me, quivering and sobbing. I held her tight for a second. All around us, gunfire was exploding and bullets were smacking the walls and singing across the nave. I whispered in her ear, *"Stay put. You're safe behind the altar. Do not move!"*

She curled up in the fetal position. I grabbed the wrought iron candelabra. It was about three feet long with a wicked spike at the top. I slid down the two steps and crawled on my belly into the side aisle, by the transept. Right there, peering from behind a pillar, taking aim at Red's men, was one of the suits. He didn't notice me because there was too much noise, and he was busy trying to kill people. I levered myself to my feet and put every ounce of rage and hatred that I had built up over the last couple of hours, all the pain, the agony and the fear, all of it, into that one, superhuman blow with the iron candelabra, that smashed his skull and snuffed out his life. Leaving a red smear on the whitewashed wall.

His piece was a 9 mm Glock. Not my favorite weapon, but efficient, and it would do the job I had in hand. I picked it up and hunkered down. I had three of Montilla's men in my line of fire. The only problem was, my hands were shaking like I had advanced Parkinson's. I took three deep breaths, propped my arms against the pillar, and took aim. Three double taps, six shots. The grouping wasn't bad. They all went down. Montilla's ten men was now just six, including himself. That meant now he was outnumbered by Red's boys.

There was a moment's panicked shouting in Montilla's gang and he dispatched two of his suits to neutralize me. I'm not easy to neutralize, and as they came around the pillar, their guns blazing, they found I wasn't there. I was over by the wall, lying in the shadows. But they never got to find out where. If I had been in full health I would have gone for headshots. But the state I was in, I aimed for the chest, double tapped and took them both down easy.

Montilla was now down to four men. I took their weapons, scrambled back to the altar and shouted at the top of my voice, "*Montilla! You're down to four men, you son of a bitch.*"

The church went silent. I gave it a beat and shouted into the void. "*Chetan! Listen to me! We take out this son of a bitch. I go my way, you go yours! We have a common enemy! We outnumber him now!*" I waited. There was more silence. I played my trump. "*Storm the bastard! I'll take him from the rear!*"

It was too much for them to resist. They were terrified of

what Montilla would do to them if he survived, and they had seen what I was capable of. They came screaming out of the pews like an army of barbarians. Montilla's four men started shooting like crazy. One of Red's men screamed and went down, so his charging horde was a total of just six. Plus Montilla's four, that was ten guys, all attacking head on. None of them was looking at me, because they were all focused on each other, and the hail of bullets that was crossing the nave of the house of God.

I used the altar to steady my arms and worked systematically. I took down two of Montilla's guys with clean headshots. That left Montilla and one of his suits. They must have been going crazy trying to work out how the hell the situation had turned so fast.

I shifted my aim. Two more of Red's charging maniacs had gone down under Montilla's hail of bullets. That left four. I took out two, and next thing Montilla and his guy and Red and Chetan were racing each other to the door. I tried to take out Chetan, but I got Montilla's guy. Then they were out, into the night. I hobbled after them. I needed Rafael Montilla and I needed him alive. I also needed Chetan dead. Red was a schmuck, but Chetan was dangerous.

I got to the door and my legs gave out under me. I heard the roar of engines and the scramble of tires on dirt, and as I crawled out, two sets of headlamps took off, with their beams playing crazy against the dark, desert sky; one toward Mexico, the other toward Tucson.

TWENTY-TWO

Somehow we made it to the Toyota Red's men had been driving. We sat in the dark cab staring out at the unreal night, the ghostly white church with its doors open, glowing softly against the black sky and the yellow light spilling out onto the dust. We could not see the carnage inside, but it screamed at us through the silence.

Cissy was in shock. She sat trembling beside me. The desert was freezing at night and her teeth were beginning to chatter. I switched on the AC and fired up the engine, then rolled across the dirt toward the blacktop.

Slowly, clarity began to seep into my mind. I knew with an almost psychic certainty where they had gone and I knew exactly what to do—how to finish this. Every inch of my body hurt. I hurt inside and out and my muscles were so spent I could barely move the pedals and the steering wheel, but I didn't care. My pain and my exhaustion were not relevant. I had to finish it tonight, and I had to finish it my way.

I didn't see the desert. A warped, distorted orange moon

was making black stencils of the mountains in the east, like something out of an apocalypse. Papago cacti leapt at us out of the darkness, into the narrow funnels of light from the headlamps. And nightmares washed around us, invisible as we raced through the night. But I ignored them all. I could see just one thing in my mind, revenge, and I kept playing it out, over and over, feeding on it, nourishing my limbs and my hatred with it.

Topawa rose, a dead glow illuminating still, silent houses and cars. We flashed through it and were gone. Then we were climbing gradually into the highlands south of Sells. The road, arrow-straight till then, began to bend and weave slightly. Then Sells was ahead of us, ghostly and still. We sped through it, past the dreaming, peaceful houses with blind, sleeping windows. And next the Ajo-Tucson Highway was there. The tires screamed as I turned east onto it and floored the pedal.

Cissy had curled up on her seat, hugging her arms and trembling. I watched the needle climb to eighty on the speedometer. For twenty minutes, we hurtled through the desert. Then we were entering Three Points and the general store and the gas station were ahead of us at the crossroads. I felt the hot burn of adrenaline fuel the rage in my belly as I skidded right onto the 286 and headed south.

South, toward Keystone and the county sheriff. My voice was loud and shocking in the dark closeness of the speeding cab. "Cissy, I need you to focus now. I need you to pay attention and answer my question. Can you do that?" I glanced at her. She was staring at me and trembling, but she nodded. "I need you to tell me where Red's uncle Caleb lives."

It took her a moment, but she finally said, "As you're coming in to Keystone, on the left, Ruggles Road. It's a quarter of a mile up, on the right. Are you going to…"

"You just stay in the car. I'm going to bring you a blanket and a hot drink. This all finishes tonight, baby."

She nodded and we drove in silence for another fifteen minutes. Then I was turning onto the Keystone Road, slowing, searching for Ruggles as the limpid glow of Keystone rose ahead of me. I found it on the left and turned, with the certainty of death in my heart. I killed the headlamps and cruised slowly till I could see the house ahead. There were lights on inside. I pulled off the road and stopped.

"Is that it?"

She nodded.

I climbed out and went the rest of the way on foot. I didn't try to be quiet. I was too tired and too mad to try to do anything. He had the drapes open and I could see them inside. The window was a warm, orange oblong in the black stencil of the house. I could see from a distance they had a fire burning. The sheriff was standing by the fireplace with his arms crossed. Red was pacing up and down. I couldn't see Chetan, but I guessed he was sitting, thinking.

I circled around the back of the house where I figured the kitchen would be. Like most back doors, the lock was a chubb and took me about fifteen seconds to pick, maybe less. I pushed it open and stepped in. The block of knives was by the cooker. I guess even slobs like Caleb cook sometimes. I pulled out the biggest blade and wondered if he kept them sharp. We'd soon find out.

I moved down the passage till I was standing outside the living room. I could hear them talking. It was mainly Red.

He was having some kind of crisis. His voice was shrill and he was panicking.

"What the fuck are we gonna do? They're gonna come for us. We pissed off the Sinaloa cartel, man! That's bad! That's *real* bad..."

The sheriff's voice drawled, "Will you git a grip of yourself, Red? You're squealin' like a girl. From what you're tellin' me, that motherfucker whipped their asses and as of right now, there ain't nobody in southern Arizona dealin' in whores and blow on any kind of scale. This ain't a problem, Red. This is an opportunity."

Chetan's rasp. "He's right, Red. You need to get a grip. You're losing it."

Caleb again. "We step into the void and take over..." He chuckled. "That asshole done us a favor."

Into the void, yes. Take over, not so much. I heard Red's boots step up to the door and stop. I moved. I opened the door, put my left forearm across his throat, squeezed and pushed the whole length of the kitchen knife through his kidneys and into his liver. He jerked and quivered for a couple of seconds, and then he was dead and all his worries were over.

Mine were just beginning.

Red slid off the knife onto the floor. The sheriff was frowning, staring at him with a 'does not compute' expression on his face. But Chetan was already on his feet, charging at me. I was weak and exhausted, and he was strong. He grabbed my wrist in his left hand and pounded my belly twice with his right fist. I went down and he was on top of me, forcing my knife hand in toward my neck and face.

I saw the sheriff take three steps toward us and stand

staring. Chetan released his right hand from my wrist and pounded my face with his fist, once, twice, but the third time I had maneuvered the blade round and gashed his left forearm. He yelled and fumbled, trying to get a better hold on my arm without letting go. He was tough but I dug deeper with the blade and he screamed and staggered to his feet.

The sheriff was reaching for his revolver. Chetan was dazed by the pain, but he was hard and he was a survivor. He lunged at me in a kick. I dodged and slashed at his leg. The blade was not sharp and did not cut. But as he came down from the kick I jabbed at his face with my left fist and as he blocked the punch I drove the knife into his chest. He made a strange wheezing, gurgling sound and I screamed and heaved and drove him backward into the sheriff.

As we collided, I let go the knife, stepped to the side and drove my right fist into the sheriff's face. He staggered back, dazed, pulling his piece from his holster. He was too slow and it was easy. I pinned his wrist against his hip and rammed the heel of my hand into the tip of his jaw, slamming his teeth together and knocking him unconscious.

I used his cuffs to pin his arms behind his back and ripped the cable out of a table lamp to tie his ankles together, loose enough for him to walk, but tight enough for him not to run.

After that, I went into the kitchen and made some coffee. I was shaking badly, but I needed to hold it together a little longer. While the coffee was brewing, I went and got a blanket. I jogged down to the Toyota with it, climbed in the cab, and wrapped it around Cissy. Then I drove up to the house, reversed to the front door and dropped the tailgate.

When I went back in, I could hear the sheriff sobbing and groaning, and repeating, "Oh, God... Oh God..."

I got the coffee, poured it into a flask with a generous dose of bourbon and took that out to Cissy. Then I went and dragged the sheriff to his feet.

"Walk, you son of a bitch."

I marched him out to the truck and shoved him in the back. There were a couple of bungies there and I used them to secure his cuffs to the back of the truck. I checked my watch. It was almost midnight.

I climbed in, fired up the engine and took off for Tucson. As I accelerated toward the 286, I reviewed the situation. Red, Chetan and their gang were all dead. Cissy was safe. I'd stop by the Hawk's Nest on the way to her house, collect my knife and my Sig, and the bag of money. That would be for Cissy, as I had promised her. I would leave her safe and sleeping, and then the sheriff and I would go back to Marni's.

Sheriff Caleb of San Juan County and I had business to attend to. Business I should have addressed from day one. Business I was going to finish now.

TWENTY-THREE

I DON'T KNOW HOW I DID IT, BUT I MANAGED TO carry Cissy into her house and up the stairs to her room. I left the bag of cash on her chair by her bed. It would be poor consolation for what she had been through, but that is the hell we live in: poor consolation. We live, we fight, we survive and win, and then at the end of it all, we die. Any victory is poor consolation in a game like that.

I went back to the truck, dragged the sheriff around to the passenger seat, and took off for Marni's place. I parked on Tamara Drive and dragged Caleb to the house with the muzzle of my Sig stuck in his ribs. I opened the door and shoved him in. We stood a moment in the dark hallway, listening. The house was silent.

He was panting and shaking. "What the hell do you think you're doing, boy? You can't get away with this..."

I cuffed him to the banisters and sprinted up the stairs to check each bedroom and the bathroom. There was no sign of Marni, or that anybody had been there at all. I went down and dragged the sheriff up to the spare room. There I cuffed him to the bed.

"Sleep. Tomorrow you are going to redeem yourself for all your sins, Sheriff. First, you are going to swear an affidavit for me, and then you are going to deliver a package. When that is done, you will have cleaned your karma and you will be a free man. You can thank me for that."

He looked at me like I was crazy. Maybe he was right. At that moment I felt pretty crazy.

I went and stood for ten minutes under a hot shower. Then I toweled myself, dressed in fresh clothes, and went down to the kitchen. There I devoured two steaks and had a large whiskey. I began to feel better, but sleepy. So I had a coffee, drafted a document and called Phil again. I needed him to do some research for me, and send some messages that would not be traceable. He came through. Phil always came through.

By four AM, I was done and I allowed myself four hours' sleep on the sofa.

At eight, I woke up and had more coffee. Then I carried a glass of milk up to the sheriff and told him to drink it all. He was still looking at me like I was crazy, and I still kind of agreed with him.

While he was drinking, I rummaged in my wardrobe and found my remaining cake of C4. I broke off a pellet about a square inch and stuffed a remote detonator in it. I put the cake in my pocket and took the pellet downstairs to the kitchen, found a pair of rubber gloves and cut off one of the fingers. I stuffed the pellet of C4 into it and sealed it with electrical tape. Then I went and cuffed the sheriff's hands behind his back again, pulled him down into the living room and made him kneel.

I showed him the pellet.

"Swallow this and I'll let you go."

He stared at it and then at me. "What is it?"

"It's none of your goddamn business what it is. I need to keep it hidden for a few hours. Swallow it and I'll un-cuff you and untie your ankles. Don't and you're no use to me, so I'll blow your brains out."

He nodded. It took him a few tries, but he eventually managed. When he'd swallowed it, I went and got him another glass of milk to help him get it all the way down. He drank it and thanked me. I smiled.

"What you just swallowed is a square inch of C4." His face drained of all color and his arms and legs started trembling. I showed him my phone. "It has a remote detonator. If I dial the number 9 three times, it will explode with enough force to blow out all your abdominal organs and cut you in half. Do you fully comprehend that?" I showed him the phone. "This has the range of any ordinary cell. You could go to Australia and I would still reach you. Do you understand?"

His jaw started to tremble and he began to weep. I untied his ankles and removed his cuffs.

"Do exactly as I say, and in a few hours you'll crap and be free. Just stay cool and try not to annoy me. C4 is very stable and very safe. Unless I dial, you're OK."

He nodded. "OK, whatever you say. Just please don't..."

"Take it easy." I stood. "Come on, we are going into town. By this evening this will all be over."

His expression was pathetic. He looked grateful.

I led him out to the truck and we drove through the morning into El Presidio and parked at La Placita Shopping Center. I left the sheriff in the truck in the parking lot and went to buy a lever arch file, a black felt pen and a giant manila envelope. Then I sat in the sun, in the gardens on El Paso Avenue, and put the lever arch file, with its contents, into the envelope and addressed it to Professor Engels, at the University of Arizona, School of Natural Resources and the Environment.

When I'd done all that, I returned to the truck. I climbed in and handed the Sheriff the envelope.

"I want you to deliver this, this afternoon, at the university."

He nodded. "OK." He looked kind of relieved. I guess he was thinking that if he delivered it, that meant he would still be alive. He swallowed. "What now?"

"Now we go to the law offices of Mathersen and Gelt, to swear an affidavit." I reached in my inside pocket for the document I had written the night before. I handed it to him. "Read it."

He took it and started reading. Then he stopped and stared at me. "Are you insane?"

"Read it!"

He coughed and read aloud.

"I, Caleb Brown, sheriff of San Juan County, Arizona, do hereby aver and swear that I have, through diligent and thorough investigation, uncovered proof positive that certain individuals within the University of Arizona, working within the School of Natural Resources and the Environment, are engaged in illegal experiments, as part of a conspiracy conducted by an organization named Omega, forming a government within the government, to exercise mind control over the population of the United States.

"These experiments are being conducted at the partially finished Biosphere 3 project, currently in construction at Buena Vista Lake, south of Beyerville, where sun beetles are being cultivated for the psychotropic, mind-altering chemicals contained in their exoskeletons.

"Experiments are also being conducted as part of Project Apollo, where human brains are being grown on rats to ascertain whether certain neural functions can be hijacked and controlled. Also involved is the Social Environmentalism Project, which is linked to the departments of Social Sciences and Psychology, to study the interaction of the environment with the collective human psyche. All of these projects have the purpose of enslaving the human population of the U.S.A. to serve Omega.

"I further aver that all three of these projects are funded with money donated by the Sinaloa drugs cartel in Mexico, through the following money laundering operations: Inversiones Sonora, based in Hermosillo, Mexico; Phoenix Investments, based in Washington DC; and R&D Funding, based in Boston, and are overseen by Rafael Montilla, a leading member of the Sinaloa cartel.

"Documentary evidence and proof of these claims is contained in a file which I have handed to Professor Engels of the University of Arizona, to be presented by him to the Federal Bureau of Investigation. I have taken these unorthodox steps because I do not know whom I can trust. Signed and sworn..." His voice trailed off. "You are. You're insane. You're one of those whacked-out conspiracy nut jobs."

"Maybe, either way you're going to sign it."

We pulled up on West Cushing outside a low, one-story building that looked like something out of a Clint Eastwood movie. We pushed through the door and the receptionist looked up and smiled at us. The sheriff smiled nervously back.

"I need to see one of the attorneys, any one of them, don't matter which, but it's real urgent. *Real* urgent. You might say it's a matter of life or death."

He didn't need to lay it on. She could see by his pale skin and his perspiration that he was sincere.

"I think Mr. Brunswick is free at the moment..." She picked up the internal phone and a couple of minutes later we were shown into Mr. Brunswick's office. He was a distinguished man with silver hair and a pencil moustache. He shook hands with us and showed us to a couple of chairs at his desk. He smiled urbanely.

"Sheriff, my receptionist tells me your matter is urgent." He frowned. "You are of course out of your jurisdiction..."

I smiled back. "Jurisdiction is not an issue here, Mr. Brunswick."

He glanced at me curiously. "Indeed, well, what is the issue?"

The sheriff took a deep breath and handed over the document. "I want... I *need* to sign this affidavit."

Brunswick started to read and frowned. He glanced up at the sheriff, settled his ass and continued reading, his frown deepening as he did so. When he had finished, he sat a moment staring at the single sheet of paper. Finally, he said, "Of course, I can't stop you from swearing this document, Sheriff..."

I gave a small cough. "Nor would it be lawful or ethical for you to attempt to do so, Mr. Brunswick. The most you *can* do is to ask the sheriff, very properly, if he is truly willing to swear to the content of that affidavit."

His face had become hostile. "I am aware of my duties, Mr. Walker. I do not need to be reminded." He sighed deeply and looked back at the sheriff with searching eyes and said, "Are you quite certain that this is what you want to do, having taken into account all the consequences?"

The sheriff nodded. "Yes."

Brunswick read the document aloud, the sheriff signed the paper, and the attorney stamped and sealed it. I said, "We are going to need a dozen official copies."

Twenty minutes later, we stepped out into the October sunshine and climbed back into the Toyota. Sheriff Caleb looked bad. I started up the truck and we drove at a steady pace to Fort Lowell Road. There are not many cyber cafes in Tucson. But there is one there, and we parked outside and went in. You could tell by the sheriff's face that he knew the whole business was coming to a head. He had the look of a man who is about to come face to face with his destiny. He wasn't wrong. He just didn't know yet what his destiny was.

We scanned the document and I attached it to eight emails. Phil had given me the necessary addresses the night before. They were the addresses of national TV and newspaper journalists who he knew would jump at a story like this. It would not be enough to blow the top off the conspiracy, not by a long shot. I was not naïve enough to believe that. But it would be enough to cause Omega hurt and worry, and maybe even force them to scupper these particular research programs. It might buy time, and it might also be enough to make Marni talk to me.

The emails named a time and a place where the sheriff swearing the attached affidavit would hand over documents probative of the conspiracy alluded to in the sworn statement, to senior academics from the School of Natural Resources and the Environment of the University of Arizona, for them to hand over in turn to the FBI. The handover would take place at four o'clock that afternoon, at the Biosphere 3 Project complex, at Buena Vista Lake, Beyerville, in the southern parking lot. It recommended they keep a discreet distance until the handover.

That left just one thing to be done.

We drove south down Campbell, toward the university. We parked outside the School of Natural Resources and the Environment and walked, through the late morning sun, toward Professor Engels' office. His secretary looked surprised, but not in a good way, to see me, and frowned at the sheriff.

"Can I help you?"

I'd primed the sheriff in the truck on what I wanted him to say. He sat, uninvited, and I sat next to him. He took out his handkerchief while she watched him, and mopped his brow.

"It's a little delicate," he said and managed to smile with his mouth while he frowned with his eyes. "I really need to see Professor Engels, quite urgently."

She gave me the dead eye and said to the sheriff, "I have already explained that he is out of town…"

He interrupted her. "Yeah, I know that, sugar, but see, you're gonna have to get him back here real fast, because his career is on the line and I am trying to save it for him. Now, I know you're trying to help him, sweet cheeks, but he ain't gonna be very grateful to you if he gets back to find he's lost his job and his reputation because you didn't want to call him on the phone."

Her face had flushed and she had gone very stiff.

"I don't *know* where he is!"

"Then here is what you are going to do." He held up the lever arch file for her to see. "In this file I have documents which could end Professor Engels' career. You understand me? So you need to get onto his colleagues—you listen real careful to me now—his colleagues on the Biosphere 3 project, Project Apollo and the Social Environmentalism Project. You got that? Write it down." She wrote it down and he went on. "You get onto them right now and tell them to get a hold of him, and bring him, urgent, to the Biosphere 3 southern parking lot, today by four PM. I'll be in a Toyota truck. And there, I will hand over these documents to him and his colleagues."

He pulled a long manila envelope from his pocket. It was an envelope I had given him earlier. It contained an official copy of his affidavit. He handed it to her. "Give this to them. If I see anybody other than Engels and his colleagues in that parking lot, that shit goes public in ten minutes flat." He nodded at her phone. "Do it, sweet cakes."

And we left.

TWENTY-FOUR

I figured it was a safe bet that Engels was in bed with Omega. It followed that his colleagues on the three Omega projects were also in bed with them. They couldn't be sure, but they had to believe there was an even chance that the documents the sheriff was talking about handing over might be Marni's father's research.

It took us slightly over an hour to get to the Biosphere, following the route I had taken with Red and his boys when we'd gone to see Romero. It seemed like a month ago, but it was only a couple of days. We headed south on the I-19 and came off at Rio Rico, going southeast along the course of the Santa Cruz river as far as Bayerville. Now, in the daylight, you could see the sprawl of the Biosphere 3 construction site, with its two vast, completed white spheres, and the third, further away in the distance, half finished.

Connecting them was an expanse of gardens, low, flat buildings, and smaller spheres and domes. It looked like a set from a 1960s sci-fi movie, sparkling white under the perfect, desert sky, with the sun reflecting off the Bella Vista lake.

Now, instead of following the road south toward the border, as we had that night, we turned east and wound down into the valley and the concrete expanse of parking lots that surrounded the complex. Finally, I came to a halt in the south lot, making sure the truck was clearly visible. I checked my watch. It was three PM.

The sheriff looked depressed. He frowned at me, searching my face. Maybe he hoped to find some compassion there.

"Tell me straight, son. Do you plan on killing me?"

"I told you already. Do as I say, follow my instructions to the letter, and this afternoon you get to go home."

He nodded. Thought about it and nodded again. "OK, thank you."

I sat a moment looking back at him, thinking about all the young girls he had helped to kidnap and sell into the white slave trade; of all the lives he had destroyed, all the happiness he had robbed from them. I climbed out. He did the same and came around to join me.

"You do this next bit on your own," I said. His eyebrows twitched. I went on, "They'll be here in about fifty minutes, maybe sooner. I want you to greet them right there..." I pointed to a spot midway between the tailgate and the hood. "It has to be exactly there, you understand?"

He nodded and stood in the spot. He wanted to be helpful. He wanted to go home. "Right here?"

"Right there, Sheriff. You let them come to you. You do not under any circumstances go to them. There will be three or four of them, maybe more. Whoever seems to be in charge, you hand them the package. They will leave and you will get in the truck and go home."

"Just like that?"

"That simple."

"OK..." There was the faint ring of hope in his voice. I held out my hand to him. "I won't be seeing you again, Sheriff. I hope you've learned something from this experience."

He took my hand and shook it. He looked confused. Maybe he was having an epiphany.

I turned and walked away from him, across the concrete, across the sidewalk, and through the glass doors into the cool, domed atrium of the southern sphere. There was a reception desk on the right. Ahead of me there was a wide space, maybe sixty or seventy yards across, with clusters of chairs and small tables covered in magazines and leaflets. Small tropical gardens dotted the area, with tall palms and ferns reaching high up toward the dome, where water vapor was released in a fine spray, down onto the plants.

I picked up a magazine and settled to wait. The big unknown now was whether the press would turn up. If Phil had been as good as his word, and so far he always had been, there would be a lot of curiosity among the journalists we had contacted. It would be interesting to see how many editors were willing to pursue the story, and how many got sat on by their bosses. It would be a test—an important test for the future.

At twenty-five minutes before four, I glanced at the sheriff. He was staring away to one side and frowning. I saw him look toward the sphere, like he wanted me to see what was going on. I got up and walked over to the glass doors. A van from a local TV channel had pulled up and the cameraman and the anchor were looking around, scanning the area. They spotted the sheriff and exchanged a few words with each other. The cameraman took up a concealed position and discreetly started filming.

I stepped out and looked around. There were a couple of cars parked nearby, and guys with cameras. Maybe they were press, maybe not. A chopper circling in the distance. Maybe.

At three forty-five, a dark blue Audi Q5 pulled into the lot. It cruised slowly for a while, like it was looking for somewhere to park. I watched the camera crew watching the Audi. Then I glanced at the chopper. It was coming closer. Suddenly, there was a whole chorus of interested spectators carefully watching while they kept their distance. Then the Audi accelerated and pulled into a space ten or twelve yards away from the sheriff. Five people got out, three men and two women. None of them was Engels, but they had that unmistakable academic look about them—ruthless geniuses prepared to go to any lengths to see their insane dreams become reality.

They closed in on the sheriff. He moved into position halfway down the truck. As I watched, their clothes began to flap and their hair began to whip this way and that. The trees behind the truck began to bow and dance in the powerful downdraft of a chopper moving in overhead. They looked up, shielding their ears and instinctively hunching their shoulders against the power of the helicopter. One of the men stepped toward the sheriff, shouting something. The sheriff grabbed the big manila parcel from the back of the truck and handed it over.

I dialed. The sheriff's detonator went off a second before the one in the parcel. His belly and his chest expanded horribly, as though he'd been pumped up with gas. His cheeks inflated grotesquely as air and gas were expelled through his mouth and nose, spraying blood and gore over the gang of professors, who screamed and cowered back. Then, the fifteen ounces of C4 that were in the box exploded, ripping those academics apart and sending bits of them flying high into the air, scattering their limbs across the parking lot.

I had been very particular about where I wanted the sheriff to stand. I had told him to position himself right by the gas tank, and now the blast ruptured it and the truck jumped six feet into the air, spraying the area with burning gasoline, igniting the dismembered academics where they lay, in pieces, on the concrete.

There was a lot of screaming and people running around like headless chickens. Security guards scrambled, talking on their radios, calling emergency services to come and do too little too late. I left by the west entrance and made my way through the gardens, watching the people swarm toward the column of black smoke that was being driven away by the blast from the rotors of the chopper above.

I chose an unremarkable car, picked the lock and hotwired it. I left the south parking lot unnoticed and headed back toward Bayerville. At Rio Rico, I crossed three patrol cars speeding toward the Biospheres with their sirens wailing and their lights flashing. On the I-19, I saw several ambulances and more cop cars all racing south through the traffic, making for the disaster area.

As I drove I allowed myself a humorless smile. I had not lied to the sheriff. I had sent him home. Home to hell, where he belonged.

I felt suddenly drained, burnt out and exhausted. The

drive north seemed to take an eternity. I finally made it into Tucson around five, dumped the car at the Hope United Methodist Church on Santa Clara Avenue and walked twenty minutes to Viva Burrito on Valencia Road and called a cab.

I had the driver drop me at the corner and walked the thirty yards to Marni's house. I was telling myself everybody was dead: Red and his gang, Arana and his gang, Romero... Only Montilla had survived, and he had no idea who I was or where I was. Cissy was at home, safe, with her money.

What I planned to do now was to pour myself a large drink, order in a pizza and watch a movie while I waited for Marni and Engels to turn up. Then we would finally resolve the problem. But till then it was pizza, whiskey and movie.

That was what I told myself as I put the key in the lock and opened the door.

TWENTY-FIVE

WHEN DEATH IS A CONSTANT PART OF YOUR LIFE, you develop an instinct for it. I don't know what it is, it's like an odorless smell that permeates the air. It's like a presence that is barely detectable to the ordinary five senses. You can't smell it, taste it or feel it on your skin, and yet you can do all three of those things. Somehow, you know it's there. And it was there as I stepped through the door. My mind raced through the list of people it could be, but they were all dead, there was nobody left.

Except Marni.

A wave of nausea flooded through me. I moved silently up the stairs. There was nothing in the bathroom, and nothing in the bedrooms. Nothing had been disturbed. There had been no ransacking, no search. I stood still and silent, listening, feeling.

I was wrecked, exhausted. Had I imagined it?

I went back down the stairs. The kitchen was empty and undisturbed, and the door was locked from the inside, as I had left it. I turned and looked down the hallway to the living room door. It was open a few inches. Had I left it like that? Dread made my skin go cold and the room seemed to rock under my feet. If she was in there, if she was dead...

I found strength from somewhere and took three strides. I shoved open the door and slammed on the light. The sofa and the armchairs were empty and untouched. The drapes were drawn across the front windows and across the French doors in the dining area at the back. They would have done that first, so that no one outside would look in and see the killing, or the body.

The body was tied to one of the dining chairs, hands and ankles. They had used wire coat hangers instead of rope or tape, to increase the pain. There was a lot of blood, mostly from where the throat had been cut, but also a lot from where the teeth had been pulled, and the fingers had been removed. The pliers were still there, lying on the carpet. It had been a bad way to die.

His head hung forward. I raised it by his hair. His eyes were squeezed closed and his mouth was badly swollen, smeared with dry blood, but he was easily recognizable as Engels.

So Engels had come back. And he'd come back to Marni's house. But where the hell was Marni? My heart gave a violent jolt in my chest. She had killed my father. Had she killed Engels, too?

I'd put my father's killing down to grief and hysteria when she'd discovered that he'd murdered her own father. But was there more to it than that? I had a flash of her in my mind, cool and calm, discussing her initiation into Omega, sitting at the table with Rho, Tau and my father, Gamma.

They were discussing the wealth and power that she would enjoy as a member.

She had wanted me to believe that it was an act, that she planned to double-cross them and expose their conspiracy once she was on the inside. And there were times when I did believe her—I had played the same game with them myself. But if it had been an act, it was a damn good act.

And then she had killed my father.

My father, who had betrayed Omega. My father, who had sought to expose and destroy them. Who had wanted to help her, to be her ally.

Was that, after all, why she had killed him? Was that why she had killed Engels, or at least colluded in his killing? *Had* she gone over? It was hard to believe. But it had been so many years since I had seen her, apart from the fleeting contact in Turret. She had come to me in London, five years ago, wanting us to be a couple. I had sent her away. I had not wanted her to be a part of my life, of what I had become. I had no idea what changes she had gone through since then.

Her father's research had put Omega at risk. The risk had been enough for them to order my father to kill him. It was not so hard to believe that, as she had started her own research, they might have moved in and taken control of her. That was, after all, their great specialization. Mind control.

I thought suddenly of the tracker. Was her rucksack upstairs? Had I seen it when I checked just now? Were her boots still there? A throb of pain in my head. I reached for the tracker. It wasn't in my pocket. Somewhere between the Hawk's Nest and the sheriff's house I must have lost it. I swore violently under my breath as another wave of exhaustion drained through my muscles.

The doorbell jarred me. It was followed by a peremptory rap on the wood. I pulled my Sig from under my arm and went to stand against the wall, beside the door.

"Who is it?"

"Lacklan, open up, we need to talk."

I knew the voice. I kept the automatic in my hand and pointed it in his face as I opened the door.

"Ben."

He had two suits behind him. They looked like freshly scrubbed quarterbacks with sandpaper hair. One was black and the other was Aryan white, like the pillars of Solomon's temple.

"That is not a nice way to greet somebody, Lacklan. Put it away. You don't need it. And if you use it, these gentlemen will drop you before you can say, 'Marni.'"

"What the fuck do you want?"

"These are agents Black and White..." He smiled and they showed me their badges. Agent Black was white and agent White was black. "May we come in?"

"What for?"

"I told you, we need to talk."

"You need to talk."

"You need to listen. Quit fucking around, Lacklan. Let us in. I know what you've got in there."

"What have I got in here?"

"Engels, or what's left of him, and a big problem. If we walk away from this door, the cops will be all over you like a rash, in minutes. Be smart for once in your damn life, will you?"

I turned and walked into the living room. I heard the door close behind me and went to the sideboard where the bottle of Bushmills stood. I poured the generous measure I'd promised myself earlier, took a long pull and fished a Pueblo out of the pack in my pocket. Ben and his pals stood in the doorway watching me as I lit up. I snapped the Zippo closed and jerked my head at Engels' mortal remains in the chair.

"You did quite a job on him. What did he do to deserve it? Fail to learn his alphabet?"

Ben gave his head a small shake. "That's not my work. My subjects talk, they don't bleed."

"Does that make you one of the good guys?"

He sighed. "Don't be infantile, Lacklan. This is Hell, there are no good guys here, only bad guys and worse guys. I'm not one of the worse guys, and neither was your father. Neither are you."

"Spare me your wisdom. If you didn't do this, who did?"

"Worse guys, from Omega."

"Why? What did they want to know?"

He narrowed his eyes, like he was trying to work me out. "Who says they wanted to know anything?"

"A punishment killing?"

"Half the point of punishment is to discourage others."

I took another slug, inhaled deeply, and asked, "What do you want, Ben? You said we need to talk. So talk."

"You're becoming a real pain in the ass."

"It's what I do. I'm good at it."

"You have to stop."

"So stop me. You have Mr. Black and Mr. White here. Stop me."

"It's not that simple."

I squinted at him through the smoke and let my smile

crawl up the left side of my face. That's my ironical side. "You want me to make it easy for you?"

"No. They want you in Washington."

I stared at him. "Who wants me in Washington?"

"Omega."

I thought about it for a moment. "Fuck them."

"Like I said. It's not that simple."

"Let me make it simple for you. Fuck you, and fuck them."

He closed his eyes a moment and sighed deeply. "You know, I like you, Lacklan. I do. And I liked your father. I'm trying to do this nicely. I don't have to, but I want to. You've had a bad few days, I know that. Let's not make things any worse. We can do this two ways. We can tazer you, cuff you and drag you there. Or you can come in a comfortable private jet, have a meal, a martini, and sleep on a comfortable couch. We'll even put you up in a five-star hotel for the night when we get there. You know? Just for once, you could do it the easy way. There is no merit in always doing things the hard way. They just want to talk to you, because you are your father's son."

I drained my glass. A martini and a meal and a five-star hotel sounded good. Maybe I'd got their attention. Maybe I could get some answers. Maybe I could find out what had happened to Marni.

I jerked my head at Engels again. "What about him?"

"We'll deal with it."

I nodded. "Give me five minutes to pack my stuff."

"We're not going anywhere without you."

TWENTY-SIX

HE WAS AS GOOD AS HIS WORD. WE BOARDED A
private jet at Tucson International Airport. After we'd taken
off, they served me two large martinis and fed me a steak.
Then they let me sleep for three hours on the leather couch.
We got to DC's Reagan National Airport at shortly before
midnight and they drove me to the Washington Hilton on
Connecticut Avenue. I ordered a bottle of Bushmills, had a
long, hot shower and lay on the bed, drinking whiskey and
watching the TV.

The news was full of the Biosphere 3 conspiracy, the
mysterious contents of the documents, and the assassination
of the sheriff and the as yet unidentified academics from the
University of Arizona.

The next morning, Ben came to collect me at ten AM.
I'd had breakfast and I was waiting for him in the lobby, with
less of a hangover than I deserved. I followed him out and
down the steps to an official limo. Our driver had that hard,
Secret Service android look, with a wire coming out of his

ear and down his collar. He probably had instructions to shoot me if I sneezed too loud.

We took the George Washington Memorial across the bridge into Virginia, and in a little more than ten minutes, we were at the Pentagon north parking lot. Ben led me to the corridor 8 entrance, where we were met by another Secret Service android in a suit with a wire in his ear, who handed us authorization badges, then led us through rings E, D and C to ring B.

From there, he took us up two floors to room 32. There he left us, and Ben knocked before opening the door and letting me into a large office about twenty-five feet square. There was a flag against one wall and a portrait of the President, there were mahogany bookcases and black leather chairs and a sofa around a coffee table. A large, oak desk stood by a window that overlooked an internal garden. I knew enough about the Pentagon to know that this location, B 32, represented power, just about as high as you can go.

There was nobody sitting behind the desk, but there was a tall man standing with his back to me, looking out of the window. He turned after Ben had closed the door, and I saw his face, but I had already recognized him.

"Rho. This is a nice office for a middle manager."

There was no humor on his face. "That's what you said last time we met, Lacklan. You described me as a guy pissing in my knickers, and called me a middle manager." He gestured around him. "There are almost eight billion people in the world. There are twenty-four letters in the ancient Greek alphabet. Each one of those letters relates to a member of the inner cabal of Omega. Twenty-four out of eight billion, and I am one of them. Middle management, Lacklan?"

"You're still a middle manager pissing your knickers, Rho. What do you want?"

He sighed deeply. "Personally? I want you dead. And if it were up to me, you would be by now. But there are men more powerful than I who want to keep you alive for now, provided you will deal with us."

"Deal?"

He pointed at a black leather armchair, part of the nest around the coffee table. "Sit. You want coffee?"

I shook my head and sat. "No. Deal how?"

He sat opposite me. Ben sat on the sofa.

"I've been watching the news. That wasn't smart. Why did you do it? Who was that sheriff?"

I smiled, enjoying his discomfort. "The sheriff was a punk in a uniform, trafficking girls and coke. Why did I do it?" I gave a small laugh. "You're all about smoke and mirrors, Rho. These stupid names you have, Tau, Rho, Omega. It's all bullshit, illusions to make you look invincible, as though you wield absolute power. Well, I thought I'd stir you up a bit and see what happens."

He and Ben were both frowning. Ben said, "What are you talking about?"

I studied his face a moment. I was genuinely surprised at the question. "Your masters claim to own the press, Ben. But there they were, with just a couple of hours notice, a chopper from one of the major networks, and a whole raft of smaller agencies." I paused, letting it sink in. "And I made sure to give Omega as much notice as the media. But they still turned up." I shrugged, turning to Rho. "And from what I could see on breakfast TV, the story hasn't died yet. Within forty-eight hours it's going to be all over social media, and you know what that means?" They didn't answer. "It means that every congressman and -woman that you don't own, every general and colonel, every politician and journalist, and every Joe in the street, is going to have a point of reference, somewhere to start digging, somewhere to meet and connect. *That* is a big part of why I did it."

They were quiet. After a moment, Rho glanced at Ben before turning his eyes on me. He was trying to look intimidating, but he just looked scared.

"After this meeting, I am going to recommend that you be terminated."

I laughed. "When you sent Ben and Brown to my house, that's what they said you were going to do. So go ahead, do it! What are you waiting for?"

"We need to find Marni, and we need to find her research. You are our simplest way of doing that. But our patience is not endless."

"Fuck you."

Ben laughed. It was a tired laugh. "You know, your father was right about you. You are one obstinate son of a bitch." He said it without hostility and I frowned at him. "Every single goddamn step has to be fought for with you, hasn't it?" He gave his head a single shake. "Can't you just for half an hour lay down your fucking battle axe and listen? Maybe, you know, just *maybe*, you are wrong."

"Wrong about what?"

"Wrong about us. Wrong about what we are trying to do. Wrong about your arrogant, opinionated, egocentric vision of the world. Just listen for half an hour. You don't have to agree, and if you don't, you can walk out of here and we'll continue trying to kill each other." He paused and they both stared at me for a while. Then Ben continued. "And if that happens, however good you are, you will lose, because there is one of you and there are hundreds of us, and we control thousands. Tens of thousands."

"Yeah? Fuck you. We all lose in the end, Ben. You know that." I sighed. "OK, I'm listening."

Rho seemed to be doing some kind of breathing exercise to keep his patience. After a moment, he said, "We have known, all major western governments have known, since the '70s, that there was no turning back as far as climate change was concerned. The cure, back then, would have been as destructive as the problem itself. Six billion people, *back then*, depended on mass production and mass distribution to survive. If we stopped using fossil fuels, that meant halting mass production and mass distribution, people worldwide would have died in their thousands of millions."

"Tell me something I don't know. Rho."

He ignored me. "The problem has grown exponentially since then. Not only are there two billion more people in the world, but we have gone well beyond the point where we could say, 'all right, we'll cease burning fossil fuels and take the consequences.' That is no longer an option. Do you understand that? I am making a point here." He gave a small, humorless laugh. "*Whatever* happens now, the outcome is irreversible. It *will* get hotter, there *will* be famine on a global scale, crops *will* fail catastrophically. Thousands of millions *will* perish. There *will be* global war, because with the population of the Earth at its maximum limit, the amount of earth—of *land*—able to sustain human life is going to shrink catastrophically in a matter of a couple of short years. *This is going to happen— very soon!*"

"What's your point?"

"My point, Lacklan, is that *there is nothing anybody can do about it!*"

I spread my hands. "OK, so we're done here."

His face flushed and he exploded. "*No! We are not done, Lacklan!*"

I sighed and pulled my cigarettes from my packet. I poked one in my mouth and lit up. I breathed smoke out of my nose and waited. I knew I was being a pain in the ass and I didn't care. I have an unreasonable dislike of people who think they own the world.

Ben leaned forward. I was surprised to see amusement in his eyes. "Humanity is not the best thing that ever happened to this planet, Lacklan. Your father understood that very well. We often talked about it. But we are not the worst thing that ever happened either. We have done good things. Maybe the greatest thing we ever did was to wake up..."

"Wake up?"

"Become conscious. The evolutionary step we took, as humans, is unique. It is..." he shrugged and shook his head, unable to find a better word to describe it. "How many billions, trillions of light-years would you have to go through space to find another self-aware species? We are a jewel in the cosmos. And brutal, fumbling and cruel as we are, we have used that consciousness to do great things. Mozart's concertos, Van Gogh's paintings, Shakespeare's sonnets and plays..."

"I get the idea. Don't patronize me."

He ignored me, stressing his point. "Democracy, the declaration of Human Rights..."

"Stop, you're going to make me vomit."

"The point is, Lacklan, that these things need to be preserved."

"And *you* are the guys to do it?"

It was Rho who answered. "Do you know of anybody else?"

I nodded. "Yeah, as it happens I do. What about the United Nations? Isn't that the kind of thing they are there for? What about getting all the heads of state in the world around the table and making a plan...?"

Ben was laughing out loud before I had finished. His amusement seemed real. Rho had sat back in his chair, sighing and looking away at the wall. He wasn't amused. I felt a rush of hot anger to my head.

"What, that's funny? Seven and a half billion people dying of disease and starvation is funny to you?"

"No." It was Rho. He looked back at me. "No, it's not funny, Lacklan. What's funny is that you—a bitter, twisted cynic like you—should be naïve enough to believe that the world's political leaders would actually get around a table together for such a noble purpose. Shall I tell you why we are a government within the government? Shall I tell you why we operate in secret, and use blackmail and the threat of death and torture to control political leaders? Do I *need* to explain?"

My anger drained away as fast as it had surged. I felt suddenly empty inside, because I knew what he was going to say, and I knew that in his position, I would do the same. "Go ahead, tell me."

"Because politicians are a breed. They are parasites who feed off sheep. They are greedy, predatory, and infinitely *stupid!* They look at this holocaust that is hurtling toward us and they think one thing, and one thing only. How can we use it to gain more power? What can we do to make sure *we* will come out top dog?"

He was right and I knew it.

"And how is what you're planning any different?"

It was Ben who replied. "Because what we plan to do is to preserve all the best that humanity has created, and we plan to create an equitable, balanced, sustainable society that will not feed off the planet as a parasite. We plan to use clean, fusion energy and keep the human population down in the low millions, so that the Earth can regenerate itself. Our ultimate aim is for the good of humanity *as part of* the planet. And frankly, our plan is the only one on the table."

"What do you want from me?"

Rho answered. "I already told you. We want you to do precisely what you are doing. Find Marni—or allow her to find you. Persuade her to work with us. We know we are not perfect." He gave a small, unamused laugh. "We are pretty much making it up as we go along, adapting to a volatile situation, and even though we have got off to a bad start, we could use people like you and Marni." He shook his head again. "We are not the enemy, Lacklan."

Ben spoke again. "You need time to think this through, and we are going to give you time to do that. But before you go, Lacklan, I want you to consider something. Where we are now, where humanity stands right now, there is no way of fixing this without going through some kind of holocaust. Whichever way we go now, there will be pain, horror and death. Every path leads through hell. So the question becomes, what is the shortest route to a place where we can heal?"

I looked into his eyes. They didn't waver. I said, "And how do Montilla and the Sinaloa drugs cartel fit into this glorious vision?"

He didn't bat an eyelid. "We take whatever support we can get. We are not squeamish. But we decide on the final outcome of all this. Maybe you should focus less on where the money comes from, and more on what it was being used for."

"Sun beetles and mind control?"

"Preservation of the Earth, and human culture." Suddenly and unexpectedly, he stood. The interview was over. "Take the time you need, a day, two, stay at the hotel, relax. It's on us. Think about what we have said. Join us, in whatever capacity you like. Your father's position is still vacant. Help us to find Marni. Help us to bring her in. Let us, please, make this right."

I stood and Rho stood, too. Ben held out his hand to me. I hesitated a moment.

"So you don't know who Marni met with when she came to DC?" They didn't answer. Their faces were expressionless, like they had somehow been switched off. "And what about Engels? I had assumed he was one of yours. So why'd you kill him? Why did you torture him?"

Ben took a deep breath. "We were using him. He didn't know that he was working for us. We tortured him to find out where Marni had gone. He didn't know."

"Why didn't you take them when they were in DC?"

He shook his head. "We didn't know where they were."

So Engels hadn't lied, and his friend in Congress was for real. I took Ben's hand and we shook. They showed me to the door.

Ben asked, "Do you need a car?"

"No, I'll take a walk."

He handed me a card. It had a personal contact number on it. "Anything you need, anything at all, contact me."

I made my way down, back along the route we had followed, from Ring B back through C, D and E, and out into the autumn sunshine. I walked about a mile to the Arlington Memorial Bridge and stood looking down at the Potomac. I lit a cigarette and stood smoking and thinking. They didn't have Marni. They didn't know where she was. But they thought she would come to me, and then they would reel us both in.

I turned and started walking across the bridge, toward DC. It was maybe four miles to the Hilton, an hour's walk. And as I walked, my mind went back to Tucson, to Marni's house. I had been exhausted and in pain, and all I could think of was that I was about to find Marni's body. That had been my whole focus. But I had been over the scene again several times, and each time I was more certain. Her rucksack and her boots were not there. They had gone.

Marni and Engels had returned together, but he had stayed when she had left. Had he given his life for her? Had they sold him the same line they had just tried to sell me, and then she had opened his eyes? It was impossible to tell. But he had stayed there and been killed, while she had got away.

My tracker was somewhere between the Hawk's Nest, San Patricio and Sheriff Caleb's house. Maybe it was shot full of holes. But I was pretty sure that Phil might have some idea of what to do.

By the time I had reached the Lincoln Memorial and started up 23rd Street toward Foggy Bottom, I had started to smile. Marni had not gone over to them, I was going to find her, and they were going to let me. Now they were playing my game.

At Washington Circle Park, I heard the ping of an email arriving on my cell. I stopped, pulled it out and thumbed the screen. My stomach lurched at a hot pellet of adrenaline. It was from Sarah Connors. I opened it. It said, simply:

What the hell have you done? Why didn't you follow to DC?

Don't miss THE STORM. The riveting sequel in the Omega Thriller series.

Scan the QR code below to purchase THE STORM.

Or go to: righthouse.com/the-storm

NOTE: flip to the very end to read an exclusive sneak peak...

DON'T MISS ANYTHING!

If you want to stay up to date on all new releases in this series, with this author, or with any of our new deals, you can do so by joining our newsletters below.

In addition, you will immediately gain access to our entire *Right House VIP Library,* which includes many riveting Mystery and Thriller novels for your enjoyment!

righthouse.com/email

(Easy to unsubscribe. No spam. Ever.)

ALSO BY BLAKE BANNER

Up to date books can be found at:
www.righthouse.com/blake-banner

ROGUE THRILLERS
Gates of Hell (Book 1)
Hell's Fury (Book 2)

ALEX MASON THRILLERS
Odin (Book 1)
Ice Cold Spy (Book 2)
Mason's Law (Book 3)
Assets and Liabilities (Book 4)
Russian Roulette (Book 5)
Executive Order (Book 6)
Dead Man Talking (Book 7)
All The King's Men (Book 8)
Flashpoint (Book 9)
Brotherhood of the Goat (Book 10)
Dead Hot (Book 11)
Blood on Megiddo (Book 12)
Son of Hell (Book 13)

HARRY BAUER THRILLER SERIES
Dead of Night (Book 1)
Dying Breath (Book 2)
The Einstaat Brief (Book 3)

Quantum Kill (Book 4)
Immortal Hate (Book 5)
The Silent Blade (Book 6)
LA: Wild Justice (Book 7)
Breath of Hell (Book 8)
Invisible Evil (Book 9)
The Shadow of Ukupacha (Book 10)
Sweet Razor Cut (Book 11)
Blood of the Innocent (Book 12)
Blood on Balthazar (Book 13)
Simple Kill (Book 14)
Riding The Devil (Book 15)
The Unavenged (Book 16)
The Devil's Vengeance (Book 17)
Bloody Retribution (Book 18)
Rogue Kill (Book 19)
Blood for Blood (Book 20)

DEAD COLD MYSTERY SERIES
An Ace and a Pair (Book 1)
Two Bare Arms (Book 2)
Garden of the Damned (Book 3)
Let Us Prey (Book 4)
The Sins of the Father (Book 5)
Strange and Sinister Path (Book 6)
The Heart to Kill (Book 7)
Unnatural Murder (Book 8)
Fire from Heaven (Book 9)
To Kill Upon A Kiss (Book 10)
Murder Most Scottish (Book 11)

The Butcher of Whitechapel (Book 12)
Little Dead Riding Hood (Book 13)
Trick or Treat (Book 14)
Blood Into Wine (Book 15)
Jack In The Box (Book 16)
The Fall Moon (Book 17)
Blood In Babylon (Book 18)
Death In Dexter (Book 19)
Mustang Sally (Book 20)
A Christmas Killing (Book 21)
Mommy's Little Killer (Book 22)
Bleed Out (Book 23)
Dead and Buried (Book 24)
In Hot Blood (Book 25)
Fallen Angels (Book 26)
Knife Edge (Book 27)
Along Came A Spider (Book 28)
Cold Blood (Book 29)
Curtain Call (Book 30)

THE OMEGA SERIES
Dawn of the Hunter (Book 1)
Double Edged Blade (Book 2)
The Storm (Book 3)
The Hand of War (Book 4)
A Harvest of Blood (Book 5)
To Rule in Hell (Book 6)
Kill: One (Book 7)
Powder Burn (Book 8)
Kill: Two (Book 9)
Unleashed (Book 10)

ABOUT US

Right House is an independent publisher created by authors for readers. We specialize in Action, Thriller, Mystery, and Crime novels.

If you enjoyed this novel, then there is a good chance you will like what else we have to offer! Please stay up to date by using any of the links below.

Join our mailing lists to stay up to date -->
righthouse.com/email
Visit our website --> righthouse.com
Contact us --> contact@righthouse.com

facebook.com/righthousebooks
x.com/righthousebooks
instagram.com/righthousebooks

EXCLUSIVE SNEAK PEAK OF...

THE STORM

CHAPTER 1

Hurricane Sarah was heading for New Orleans. It was the only interesting thing the news had told me since early October; since my meeting with Omega in Washington, since that last cryptic message from Marni, asking why the hell I hadn't followed her from Tucson to Washington[1]. Since then, for almost two months, she'd fallen off the radar. There had been no clue, no message, no contact at all about where she was or what she was doing. I'd promised my father on his deathbed that I would look after her and protect her from Omega, but so far she had made that almost impossible.

And then there was the hurricane.

It was the largest and most violent in recorded history—almost a thousand miles in diameter—with winds reaching 230 MPH, surging in off the Atlantic and headed for New Orleans. And it was out of season, striking in late

---

1. □ See *Double-Edged Blade*

November, which was practically unheard of. Hurricane season was August and September.

Omega's purpose was to exploit climate change and overpopulation, in order to consolidate their global, political power. Marni's self-imposed mission was to expose Omega and bring them down. That was why she had murdered my father, that was why the Biosphere Projects had drawn her to Tucson. So maybe, just maybe, hurricane Sarah might draw her to New Orleans. It was a long shot, but it was the only shot I had right then.

So I'd called Kenny, the butler I had inherited from my father, and had him send the Zombie 222, my converted '68 Mustang, down from Weston to DC, with a kit bag in the trunk. It was sixteen hours to the Big Easy, following the I-81 and then the I-59 from Chattanooga. I wasn't sure what I was going to do when I got there. I had a few ideas—contact the Coastal Protection and Restoration Authority (CPRA), check out the university's Climatology and Earth Sciences departments, see if she had been in touch with them or any of their professors. That was the sort of direction my mind was taking. But that was before I reached Laurel, Mississipi. At Laurel, everything changed.

I had stopped at the Exxon service station at exit thirty-five, just south of the town. It was eight AM and I'd sat by the window with a large coffee and a couple of donuts. The sun had been up for an hour and a half, but outside, the sky was heavy with dark gray clouds, and the tall pines across the road were bowing and tossing in a wind that wanted to get rough.

Whoever had been at that table before me had come from Louisiana. There was a copy of the *Baton Rouge Advo-*

cate on the table. So after I'd got bored of watching the bowing pines and the random drops of desultory rain splat on the window, I pulled over the paper and turned to the front page. And that was when everything changed.

It changed because I was staring at the face of my friend and comrade in arms, Bat Hays.

I was nineteen when my parents divorced and, to get away from my father, whom I hated with a passion, I had joined the British SAS. For ten years, that had been my life. I had left, a couple of years back, aged thirty, with the rank of captain and a handful of friends who were more than brothers; men who would give their lives for me, and I for them. Bat Hays was one. Now he was staring at me from the front page of the *Advocate* with his hands cuffed behind his back.

His black, obstinate, proud face stared at the crowd as he was led by cops to a patrol car. Nobody would see the fear he felt. Nobody but me. This guy who had faced death a hundred times and laughed at it with his Cockney humor, would be completely lost and helpless in the jaws of the relentless system of the law.

The headline said:

MAN ARRESTED IN SARAH CARMICHAEL MURDER

I read on. "Bartholomew Hays, 30, originally from London, England, was arrested yesterday and charged with the murder of Sarah Carmichael, of Burgundy, in the parish of West Feliciana. Mrs. Carmichael was found shot to death in her bed by her husband, real estate magnate Charles Carmichael, on the night of Friday, 3rd November, shortly before midnight.

"The Killer fled after he was disturbed by Carmichael on

his return from dining at a restaurant. Shots were exchanged but the killer escaped through a window into the woods..."

I stepped out into the drizzle, under the lowering sky, and climbed into the Zombie. I hit the ignition and the powerful, dual electric engines kicked in. There was no roar, no thunder, no sound at all. This machine delivers eight hundred bhp, one thousand eight-hundred foot-pounds of torque straight to the back wheels, and will go 0-60 in just over one and a half seconds. But she is totally silent.

I lit a Camel, pulled quietly out of the lot, and took the 84 west as far as Natchez. It was one hundred and thirty miles, and I did it in just over an hour. At Natchez, I took Route 61 south, through Burgundy and Hardwood, to St Francisville, where the Parish Jail was. All the way, the sky loomed, darkening and lead-heavy over the green wood-lands, and the wind tossed and twisted the trees.

I found the Clerk of Court, an elegant 18th century red brick building with a pretty dome, on Prosperity Street. I was directed to the bail office, paid Hayes' three thousand five-hundred bail in cash, and headed back up Myrtle Hill Drive to the parish jail. It wasn't hard to find, though it didn't look much like a jail. It looked more like a golf club, set among green lawns and attractive, modern buildings. I figured it was part of the enlightened movement to ensure that criminals did not feel like social outcasts. I could think of several cheaper ways of achieving the same end, but then, I'm a social outcast.

I left the Zombie out front. The tropical, humid heat made it feel like late August or September, and in the time it took to cross the parking lot, I already had damp patches on my shirt. I pushed through the big glass doors into what looked like a hotel reception and told the guy on the desk who I was and why I was there. He made the call and twenty minutes later Bat, six foot two of solid muscle with an army kit bag over his shoulder, was brought out. He stopped dead in his tracks when he saw me.

"What the fuck...?"

"Hello Bat, what have you been up to?"

"What the fuck...? How the fuckin'...? Where the... *Fuck...!*"

I smiled and slapped him on the shoulder. If he'd been a fellow American, we would have embraced, but Brits don't do that. We grinned and shook hands and that was enough. It was good to see a friend.

"I see your vocabulary hasn't improved."

He laughed. "Am I glad to see you, sir! Everyone 'round here's gone stark fucking bonkers. How did you know...?"

"Come on, I'll explain in the car."

We stepped outside. The humidity had turned into a warm drizzle that dried as soon as it landed. We crossed to the car, climbed in, and slammed the doors, closing out the ominous presence of the weather. I fired up the engines and, as we pulled away, I asked him, "You got a pad?"

"Yeah, mate. I got a nice little place on Congress Street. Up in Burgundy. Nice fuckin' ride! Why don't it make no noise, though?"

I raised an eyebrow at him as we slipped silently onto Route 61 and headed north toward the small town of Burgundy. I tossed him my pack of Camels and handed him my Zippo. He took them both gratefully and as he lit up, I said, "You have some explaining to do, pal."

He inhaled deep and blew smoke at the ceiling, then lay back and closed his eyes.

"You ain't fuckin' joking, Captain. But I need somebody to explain it to me first."

"I know the answer, Bat, but I have to ask, you understand that, right?"

He nodded.

"Did you kill her?"

"You know me, Cap. I couldn't. Not a woman. Besides, I'm done with all that."

"All what?"

"Violence, killin'. Done it. Done it with the best. Got the fuckin' T-shirt. Don't want it no more. I want to do something else with me life. Know what I mean?"

"I know what you mean. Why didn't you call me?"

He looked reproachful. "Where? You fuckin' disappeared, didn't you?—sir! Nobody knew where you'd gone. Sarge said you'd gone to Wyoming, but nobody was sure. He didn't know where in fuckin' Wyoming. Wyoming's a big fuckin' place. It's like a country!"

"Bradley? The Kiwi?"

He grinned. "Yeah, old fucker. He's still with the Regiment. He'll never quit. They won't let him." He was quiet for a bit, thinking. "How'd you know I was here?"

"I didn't. I was headed for New Orleans. I saw your picture in the paper. You're famous."

"Infamous, more like."

"Who was Sarah Carmichael?"

"Wife of the local big wig. Got a reputation for being some kind of angel, concerned about the environment, helped the poor, good works. You know the kind of thing.

Hubby's a land developer. Got a big mansion in the woods outside Burgundy."

"You knew her?"

He shrugged and I knew he was going to lie to me. "She came into the club a few times."

"Club?"

"I work as a bouncer at a local club, sir..."

"We're not in the Regiment anymore, Bat. Call me Lacklan."

"I'll try. Anyway, I work as a bouncer at the Blue Lagoon, in Burgundy. They have live jazz. I play the trumpet sometimes..."

"Yeah, I remember. You were good. So...?"

"She'd come in some nights, have a drink, listen to the music."

"With her husband?"

"Sometimes."

"But not always?"

He sighed, noisily. "Yeah. Not always."

"So you talk to her?"

"Look, Cap, I know what you're drivin' at. But she was just an independent woman, who liked jazz, and would go out sometimes of an evening, sometimes in company, sometimes alone. People talk. Especially in a small, religious community like this. But she was sophisticated, intelligent. She liked the music and sometimes she'd come alone. And she'd always leave alone. No big deal."

I nodded. "OK, Bat. I'm going to get you an attorney. We'll get you off these charges."

"I can't afford it, sir."

"I can. We'll think of a way for you to pay me back. The money isn't a problem. Saving your ass is."

He nodded. "Thanks."

I gave it a moment, and as we approached Burgundy, I said, "You don't have to tell me everything, at least not yet. But when your attorney gets here, you'll have to tell *him* everything, in detail, warts and all. You understand me? Because if you don't, whatever lies you tell, will trip you up and bite you in the ass down the line. And after that, I'll beat seven bails of shit out of you." I looked him in the eye. His eyes were hard and stubborn. "They still have the death penalty here, you know that, right?"

"Yeah, I know."

"And a black Brit killing a white American woman? That's not good. Be smart. Not for me, for you."

"Gotcha."

Burgundy was one of the old towns. The streets in the outskirts were broad and leafy. The houses were Creole, one and two story clapboard, painted in many colors, red, white, blue, mauve, and green—often on a single house. There were broad gardens and a superabundance of trees. Downtown the streets were narrower, and the houses were interspersed with larger, stone buildings with wrought iron balconies and tall green and blue shutters in the French style. As we moved through the town, the bright colors, the buildings, and the narrow streets with their carnival flavor of mardi gras were strangely at odds with the dull weight of the clouds and the damp, claustrophobic heat.

I found Congress Street and he pointed me to a bright green, one-story house with a gable roof. "That's us, sir."

"You got a hotel near here?"

He frowned. "You can stay with me, Cap."

I pulled up outside his door and shook my head. "As far as Carmichael, local law enforcement, the courts, and Burgundy are concerned, I am just your commanding officer. I'm concerned for you and, above all, for the reputation of the Regiment. Drop your kit bag, we'll find a hotel, have some lunch, and then you tell me what happened."

He nodded. "Yeah, got it."

I watched him go inside through the windshield. He was one of the most dangerous men I had ever met, but right then, he looked oddly vulnerable. I looked up at the blackening sky. Under that sky, the whole world looked vulnerable.

CHAPTER 2

THE HOTEL SONIAT WAS A COUPLE OF STREETS away on Chartres Avenue. It was an old, colonial building constructed around a central patio with a fountain in the middle, four orange trees and galleried landings on the second and third floors, where the rooms were. A guy on reception with a pencil moustache, a film of sweat on his forehead, and heavy glasses told me his name was Luis and the dining room was open. We followed his directions through an arch and into a second patio, where the walls were covered in jasmine and there were geraniums growing out of artfully broken pots.

The place was empty and a bored-looking waiter greeted us with ill-concealed surprise. He showed us to a table under a creaking, hundred-year-old ceiling fan. They had air conditioning, but with an empty hotel and an equally empty restaurant, they were not about to turn it on.

"The storm is coming," he said. "They never come this far inland, but the media..." He shrugged, like the name said it all. "The town is almost deserted. We're all hoping it will turn north and blow itself out over the Atlantic, but it ain't looking good. Some people are evacuating already."

We ordered a couple of martinis and a couple of steaks and he went away to get them. I watched Bat while he studied the dining room in minute detail. Suddenly, he said, "That storm's something, ain't it? They say it's the biggest in recorded history."

I gave him a moment. He continued his minute study of the walls. Finally, I sighed loudly.

"Quit stalling, Bat. What happened?"

He puffed out his cheeks and blew, balled his fists on the tablecloth and stared down at them.

"I don't know, sir, Lacklan, mate." He looked at me with wide eyes and shrugged. "Cross my fuckin' heart and hope to die."

"What? You don't trust me?"

"Don't talk stupid. Sir. Of course I trust you. I'm just..." He spread his hands. "One minute I was workin' at the club, minding me own business, and the next minute, Detective fuckin' Jackson of the Burgundy fuckin' Police Department is arresting me for the murder of Sarah..." He hesitated fractionally and added, "Carmichael."

I watched at him for a moment, trying to read his face. Meanwhile, he studied his hands and sucked his teeth.

"You know what, Bat? I'm getting mad. I have serious business to attend to in New Orleans. I came here, like you would have come for me, like any of us would. But now I'm here and you're stonewalling me. I should tell you to go fuck yourself, and leave."

He frowned a small frown and flattened out his hands,

like looking at the back of them might give him a different perspective. After a moment, he said, "It was Friday, 10th of November, a week after she was killed. Detective Jackson come 'round to my gaff, hammering on the door, wanting to talk to me. I let him in and offered him a cup of tea, like you do, and he starts askin' me questions about Sarah Carmichael. Did I know her? Where from? How well did I know her? Did I know her husband? All that kind of stuff. Had I seen her hangin' out with anyone? Anyone comin' on to her or getting aggressive with her?

"I told him what I told you. I worked at the club. She come in sometimes to listen to the music. I knew her to say hello, never saw nothing special, no more than that. He asks if he can take my prints. I had nothing to hide so I says yeah, and he takes my prints with a mobile scanner. After that, he buggers off, and I thought that was the last of it. To be honest, Cap, I thought it was just routine stuff. I'd expected it after I heard she'd been murdered.

"But couple of days ago he turns up again..." He gave his head a little shake. "I couldn't believe it. He says he's arresting me for her murder. I says, 'On what grounds?' He says, 'On the grounds we got your fuckin' prints on the murder weapon!'"

Our drinks arrived and after the waiter had gone, we drank to old friends. He smacked his lips and sighed, then went on.

"Like I said, I couldn't fuckin' believe it, sir." He shook his head at the table top. "It's got to be a mistake. I told them that in the interrogation, 'There's got to be a mistake,' but Jackson says, 'No, mate. These modern scanners don't make fuckin' mistakes, do they? They are one hundred percent accurate.' So I'm fuckin' screwed. And what I want to know is, how my fuckin' prints got on the murder weapon. It don't make no sense."

"That's what I'm wondering."

"Yeah, well, well you might, sir, but it gets better, because not only are my prints on the fuckin' weapon, they are at the scene an' all, in the bedroom and in the livin' room. And I ain't never been to that house."

"Have you got a theory?"

He sat back in his chair with a face that said he had, but he didn't want to tell me about it because I wouldn't believe him. "It's far-fetched, but it's the only thing I can think of. You probably won't believe me. I wouldn't."

"Try me."

He picked up his glass and swirled it around for a bit, examining the ice and the olive as he did so.

"First week of October. Must've been the Wednesday, 'cause I was playin' in the band that night. Bloke come in. Flash git, sharp suit, oiled hair all shiny. Nasty piece of work, you could tell. Really white teeth, kind of blindin', always smilin', smooth, too smooth. Know what I mean? Black guy, must've been six three or four, taller than me. Anyway, he comes in and while I'm playin', I can see him having a natter with Harry, the barman. And I can see Harry lookin' at me and tellin' him something. You know, like he's tellin' him something about me."

He paused to sip his drink.

"I never tell nobody about the Regiment. But Harry helped me out couple of years ago when I was in trouble, we become mates, so I told him once. Never told nobody else. But now Harry's gone and told this sleazy geezer. So when

I've finished me set, I go to the bar to get a beer and this bloke comes up."

"The tall guy who'd been talking to Harry?"

"Yeah. Says his name is Ivory. On account of his teeth, I suppose."

The waiter brought out our steaks, set them in front of us and wished us a healthy appetite in French, and withdrew. We ate in silence for a bit, then Bat went on.

"Anyhow, so I'm having me beer at the bar and Ivory comes over and introduces himself. He was so fuckin' tall an' thin, with these shifty fuckin' eyes, it was like talkin' to a fuckin' snake. He says he's recruiting for a job, the pay is superb and am I interested? So I tell him, that depends on what the job is, don't it? And *he* says, he can't tell me. His boss would have to tell me." He spread his hands to accompany his ironic smile. "Well, I know straight away it's something dodgy, right? And I tell him I ain't interested. Then he tells me how much it pays."

He stopped and cut into his steak.

I said, "How much?"

"Twenty grand for a day's work."

"It was a hit."

"I don't know."

"That kind of fee? It was a hit."

"Probably."

"What did you do?"

"I asked him if it was a hit. He told me again that I'd have to discuss it with his employer." He made a 'whatcha gonna do?' face. "I ain't flush, know what I mean? I could use a bit of the old spondulix. So I think, no harm in talkin', and I tell the bloke, OK, take me to your leader."

He paused, stuffed a chunk of meat in his mouth, and talked around it while he ate.

"That's when it got a bit weird."

"Weird how?"

"He makes a call on his mobile—his cell phone. Then he tells me to follow him. We go outside. It's late, 'bout two AM, and we're standin' on the pavement, fuckin' sidewalk as you call it, and he gives me a fag. We're lightin' up and this big fuckin' black Lincoln comes 'round the corner from Main Street and pulls up in front of us. Two big fellas get out, in suits. One of 'em's black, the other looks Swedish, know what I mean? Blond, big 'tash. And the blond one says, 'We gotta put a bag over your head.'"

He burst out laughing and I smiled at the thought of anyone trying to put a bag over Bat Hays' head.

"You can imagine, right? After fuckin' Iraq and Afghanistan, *and* fuckin' Palestine. So I says, 'No thanks, mate. Forget it.' So Ivory is really apologetic and says it's just to protect the identity of his employer, and the fee is to make up for the inconvenience. And also, they will pay me an extra two grand, in cash, that night to compensate me. My hands will be free at all times.

"So I'm thinking, twenty grand—and I could *really* use twenty grand right now. So I agree. We got in the car. They put a bag over my head and we drove. I tried to keep track. Towns here are all on a fuckin' grid system, ain't they? So I'm doing the old 'Right, right, left, straight for two minutes...' But they're cute to me so they're goin' all 'round the fuckin' shop to put me off, and I lost track. We ended up outside the town. When we got out of the car, it was very quiet, very still. The ground was rough, gritty, like old tarmacadam that's crumbling, and there was an echo, like there was tall buildings nearby. We went through a door and my guess is that it was a warehouse or a hangar. It had that kind of echo to it, like a vaulted ceiling in a church. You know the kind of thing."

I nodded. "Yeah."

"So we crossed a concrete floor and you could tell by the sound that it was a big, empty space indoors, and they sit me on a wooden box. There's a wooden table in front of me. There's some muttering, and then this muffled voice says, 'Mr. Hays, forgive all the cloak and dagger stuff, but I'm afraid it is necessary.' He talks a bit posh, at least, posh for a Yank. You know what I mean, don't you?" I said I did and he continued. "So he says, 'I am going to remove your hood, but before I do, I'd like to give you a small test. I hope you don't mind. I think the fee warrants it.' So I tell him I don't mind. I hear a couple of clunks on the table and he tells me there are two pistols there, and he would like to know if I can identify them...'"

"Shit. And you did..."

"Thinkin' back, it was stupid. But hindsight makes us all smarter than we really are, dunnit? I suppose I was thinkin' of the money, and I had no idea then what was going to go down later, did I?" He shrugged. "It's no excuse, I know. I picked up both guns, handled them, felt them all over. One was a Colt revolver, 38. The other was a Colt 45 automatic." He took a deep breath. "She was shot with a .38. Must have been the same one."

"You told the cops about this?"

"Yeah, but obviously they don't believe me. Who would? I wouldn't."

"It's elaborate."

"Yeah. Careful planning—and well in advance."

"At least three guys involved."

"Yeah, the guy who spoke could have been Ivory or one of the other two. The voice was muffled."

"So what happened next?"

"They removed the hood. It was very dark. There was a table in front of me but the two pistols were gone. Other side of the table there was a bloke. I couldn't make out any details. It was just a shadow. There was nobody else there. And the same voice what had spoken earlier says, 'We have a contract to offer the right person, and we understand you have experience in special operations.' I says, 'What kind of contract?' He says, 'It's a hit. You'll be given the details if you accept. It pays twenty thousand dollars.' So I tell him, 'Thanks, but no thanks. I was a soldier, I ain't no assassin.' They put the hood back on and we were done there.

"I thought there might be some trouble. They might want to get rid of the witness, but there weren't. Now I know why. They took me back to the car and delivered me home, with two grand stuffed in my pocket. I had a bad feeling at first, but nothing come of it, so I forgot about it. Till now."

The waiter cleared away the plates and I ordered two Irish whiskeys. We waited in silence for him to deliver them. When he'd gone, I took a swig and let it settle, warm in my belly.

"You fucked up pretty bad."

"Don't I know it?"

"OK, so here is what we are going to do. I'm going to get the best criminal attorney in Baton Rouge. I'm going to have him come over and we'll have a conference with him. Meantime, I'm going to talk to Carmichael and Jackson. Maybe we can make them see sense."

"You don't believe I done it, do you, Captain?"

"I know you didn't."

He smiled. "How come?"

He knew the answer, but he wanted to hear it. "If you'd done it, they'd never have caught you."

He stared at me for a long moment, then raised his glass to me. "Cheers, sir. I appreciate it."

CHAPTER 3

I phoned the Advocate while we were sitting over our whiskeys and spoke to their crime and legal editor. He gave me the name of Louisiana's leading criminal advocate, David Hirschfield. "This guy," he'd said, "leaves no closet unrifled and no nose un-bloodied. He's a monster, a scary man."

He sounded like my kind of guy. I called his office and got his secretary.

"I'm afraid Mr. Hirschfield has a full caseload at the moment. It is quite out of the question."

"I will double his fee."

There was a small, patronizing laugh. "Believe me, Mr. Walker, money is not the issue. Mr. Hirschfield has some very powerful clients and he can't simply palm them off to a junior."

"Can I talk to him in person?"

"Mr. Walker, as I have said to you, he is *far-too-busy*."

She punctuated the words in order to drive them home.

I could feel the anger rising inside me. "No. You don't understand. I am going to employ Hirschfield. There are no two ways about this."

"*Mr.* Walker! I have already *told* you that it is out of the question! Now kindly…"

I thought about it for a full second, then took a decision I knew in time I would regret. But I figured I'd regret it when the time came. I interrupted her.

"I want you to listen very carefully to me," I said. "Mr. Hirschfield was recommended to me by a friend at the Pentagon…" She gave a splutter that told me what she thought of that. I continued regardless. "I am going to give you a phone number to call so that you can confirm that, and I will pay whatever Mr. Hirschfield cares to charge. But I need *him*, and I need him *now*. I will give you half an hour, and then I expect him to call me back in person. Is that understood?"

She had gone very quiet. I gave her Ben's number. Bat was staring at me like he was wondering what was in the whiskey. I hung up and called Ben's number. It rang once.

"Lacklan. I am surprised to hear from you. What's up?"

"I know I am going to regret this, Ben, but I need a favor."

"Name it. I promise you will not regret it."

I told him about Hirschfield and he went real quiet.

"What do you need a criminal attorney for, Lacklan?"

"I don't want you involved in this."

"I'm already involved. It's too late for that. Is it for you? What have you done?"

"No. It's a colleague. I've got it covered. I just need Hirschfield on board."

"A colleague? From the SAS?"

I sighed. I could sense him making signs at somebody.

"Tell me what it's about."

"I told you, I don't want you involved. Hirschfield's secretary is going to call you..."

"No, she's not. I'm going to call Hirschfield. He'll take care of your case. But there is a simpler way of doing this. I'll call the DA and have them drop the case."

"No. Just talk to Hirschfield, then stay the hell out of it."

"Fine. You understand you do not owe me personally, you owe Omega."

"I understand that."

"You won't regret it. Expect his call."

I hung up.

Bat was staring into his glass. "I remember you said your dad was a big shot."

"My dad is dead. It's best you don't know about this."

He held my eye. "I don't want you owing favors on my behalf, sir."

"Lacklan. We're friends. It's done. Forget it." I smiled. "Now you owe me."

I didn't have to wait half an hour. Five minutes later, my cell rang.

"Mr. Walker?"

"Speaking."

"You have some powerful friends."

"Mr. Hirschfield?"

"Call me David and I'll call you Lacklan. You promised to double my fee and you shall. I shall probably be in trouble with the Mob because of this." He laughed loudly. "But it pays to keep our friends in Washington happy. Now, tell me how I can help you."

"I need you to win an unwinnable case."

"That's what I do."

I gave him a rough outline. "I need you here in Burgundy by tomorrow."

He was silent a moment. "The Carmichael case, is it? I'll be there tonight. You are aware there is a storm coming, aren't you?" He sighed noisily. "But, Mr. Walker, from what you've told me so far, I can't make any guarantees as to the outcome."

"You do your best. I'll do the rest."

He shrugged with his voice. "Fair enough. Tell me where you're staying. I'll book a room."

I told him and hung up, watching Bat across the table.

"What do you know about Carmichael?"

"Not a lot. Filthy rich. Deals in real estate. People say he doted on his wife. They were married for about five years. He was a lot older than her."

"Office in town?"

He hesitated. "I think he works from home."

I raised an eyebrow at him. "She tell you that?"

"She might have mentioned something."

"How close did you get to her, Bat?"

"Look, leave it out, will ya?"

I stood. "OK, I'm going to talk to Carmichael. Try to stay out of trouble, at least till I get back."

"I'll do me best."

In the lobby, Luis was watching a small TV behind his desk. I caught a glimpse of a brightly colored weather map with a giant white spiral in the middle. It looked as though Sarah was making landfall on the Bahamas.

One Sarah was dead, but the other, it seemed, was very much alive. I drove, under a low and dangerous sky, through empty streets out of town and onto Route 61. Then I headed south, toward Hardwood and St. Francisville, for a quarter of a mile.

The gate to his property was set back from the road. I slipped through it and moved down the long driveway, through rich green lawns and an abundance of river birches, red oaks, and southern pines. They looked oddly luminous in the gloom, against the watercolor sky.

His house was a large, colonial mansion in the Georgian style, with stone Grecian columns and a gabled portico. Two broad steps led up from the gravel drive to the door. I parked, climbed the steps and rang the bell. The door was opened after a minute by a pretty maid in a uniform. I told her who I was and said I needed to see Charles Carmichael.

She went away, came back a minute later, and led me across a vaulted hall with a checkerboard floor to double walnut doors. She knocked, poked her head in and said, "Mr. Walker to see you, sir." Then she stood back to let me in.

His library-cum-office was what you'd expect, having seen the façade of his house, and his hall. It was the deep south at its most elegant. The walls were lined with dark wood panels and shelves loaded with heavy tomes. The rugs looked Persian and there was a nest of Chesterfields set around a cold fireplace.

When I went in, he was standing by a heavy oak desk to the left of the door. He was in his late fifties, with graying, well cut hair and a suit of the same color. He had his arms crossed and he did not look happy. He didn't waste time.

"Who are you?"

"Former Captain Lacklan Walker, I was Bartholomew Hays' commanding officer in the British Army."

"You're an American."

"My mother is English."

"What do you want?"

"I'd like to talk to you about what happened."

"Why?"

I sighed. "Mr. Carmichael, I am not here as an enemy. I have reason to believe that Hays did not kill your wife. If I am right and he is convicted, your wife's killer will go unpunished."

He scowled at me. "What you mean is that you want to protect the honor of your regiment."

I studied him a moment, his posture, the set of his jaw. "Are you a military man, Mr. Carmichael?"

"Yes. Marine Corps."

"Then I won't waste your time and mine by lying to you. Of course I care about the reputation of my regiment. And of course I care about a soldier who served under me with honor and courage. But not to the exclusion of all else. If he did this, then he must be punished. But if he did not..."

"He did it. His prints are in her bedroom and in my drawing room. His prints are on the gun, God damn it!"

"I have reason..."

His face flushed and he took a step toward me. "How dare you! Reason? What possible reason? You come into my house, wanting to enlist my help to protect the man who *murdered* my wife!"

I stood my ground.

"What reason? Putting it bluntly sir, if Hays had done it, his prints wouldn't be all over your house, or on the weapon. They wouldn't have the weapon, and they wouldn't have him in custody."

"Get out of my house before I call the sheriff and have you thrown in jail!"

"On what charge?"

"Trespass—and complicity in murder!"

I held his eye for a beat. "I'm going to let that pass because I can see the pain you're in, Carmichael. But the man who killed your wife is walking free, and if Hays goes down for it, your wife's killer will have got away with murder. Think about it."

His voice was cold and steady and his eyes were hard. He repeated, "Get out."

I nodded and left.

Outside, back under the heavy cloud, I paused by my car to light up a Camel and think about what I would do next. It had to be Detective Jackson, but judging by Carmichael's reaction, I didn't expect him to be very receptive.

The cop shop was at the other end of town, on Bordeaux Street. It was a small, modern building with a big parking lot and a big radio antenna. There were four patrol vehicles and a couple of unmarked cars. You got the impression they were normally busy, but did most of their work on the streets, where they didn't have to record it. Right now, it was quiet. I guessed the slow, steady exodus continued, and the people who were here were staying indoors.

I parked by the entrance and went inside. There was a bored-looking sergeant at the desk, watching the news.

Hurricane-force gales were battering the Bahamas and there was footage of palm trees bent almost horizontal as the spray from giant waves drowned them. He glanced at me and made a question with his face, while he kept one eye on the news.

"I need to talk to Detective Jackson, about the Bartholomew Hays case."

He sighed like I was being unnecessarily demanding and made a call on the internal phone, then continued watching the news like I wasn't there. A minute later, Detective Jackson stepped out in shirt sleeves with a loosened tie. He was a big man, not tall but big, with balding black hair turning to gray at the temples, and thick stubble where he was either growing a beard or he'd forgotten to shave. His eyes were dark and suspicious and examined me a moment before he spoke.

"You have information about Bartholomew Hays?"

I nodded. "Yeah. Can we talk somewhere?"

He held the door for me and led me through to his office. It was small and functional. "Take a seat."

He sat behind his desk and I sat across from him. "My name is Lacklan Walker, I was Hayes' superior officer in his regiment in the U.K. I know him as well as anybody. He served on a number of operations with me. I am pretty sure he did not commit this murder."

His only reaction was to blink, once. "You been to see Mr. Carmichael, right?"

"He called you?"

"Yeah, he said you might try to come and see me. I was expecting you. I am going to say the same thing to you as he did. Hays' prints are at the scene and they are on the weapon. You are wasting your time and, more important, you are wasting *my* time."

"You don't even want to hear what I have to say?"

He gave a small, humorless laugh. "What can you say, man? Can you explain to me how his prints appeared in the Carmichaels' bedroom?"

I shook my head. "No."

"Can you tell me how they appeared downstairs in the living room, where he has supposedly never been?"

"No, I can't."

He leaned forward and pointed at me. "Can you explain how his prints got on the murder weapon?"

"Maybe."

He shook his head. "Uh-uh, no you can't. There is no maybe. Either you can or you can't. And you—can't. And if you can't explain those three things, you are wasting my time."

"Bartholomew Hays did not kill Sarah Carmichael."

"Can you prove that?"

"Not yet."

He narrowed his eyes at me. "What do you mean, not yet?"

"I plan to find out who killed her." I smiled and gave my head a small shake. "Bat Hays is one of the most skilled assassins you are ever likely to meet, Detective. I know because I have seen him work. I know he didn't kill Sarah Carmichael *because* his prints are at the scene."

"That is bullshit."

I shrugged. "Suit yourself."

I stood and he pointed up at me. "Stay out of my way, Walker, or I'll run you in for obstruction of justice."

I put my most patronizing smile on the right side of my face. "Save it for somebody who might believe you, Jackson. You just stumbled into a bigger league."

I went out and looked up at the sky. It was early afternoon, but it was as dark as evening. A gust of wind whipped my hair and howled through the pines across the road, making them bend and creak. Sarah was going to be trouble. Sarah was going to cause havoc.

Scan the QR code below to purchase THE STORM.
Or go to: righthouse.com/the-storm